MELODY JONES

Other books by the same author

Fiction
  A Family Album
  Lamaar Ransom: Private Eye
Criticism
  The Absurd Hero
  Henry James: The Portrait of a Lady
  Edward Lewis Wallant
Editions
Critical Editions
  Pioneering in Art Collecting
  Ten Modern American Short Stories
  The Selected Writings of Edgar Allan Poe

MELODY JONES

David Galloway

JOHN CALDER · LONDON
RIVERRUN PRESS INC · NEW YORK

First published in Great Britain, 1980, by
John Calder (Publishers) Ltd
18 Brewer Street, London W1R 4AS
and in the U.S.A., 1980, by
riverrun press Inc.
175 Fifth Avenue, New York, N.Y. 10010

Originally published in Great Britain, 1976, by
John Calder (Publishers) Ltd, in
New Writers 12

British Library Cataloguing in Publication Data

Galloway, David, *b.* 1937
    Melody Jones.—(Riverrun writers).
    I. Title
    823'.9' 1F   PS 3557.A4155M/   79–41584

    ISBN 0 7145 3807 8   hardback

Typeset by Gloucester Typesetting Co. Ltd, in 11pt Bembo
Printed and bound by The Hunter Rose Company Ltd, Toronto, Canada.

CONTENTS

1   *Melody*   9

2   *Brenda*   22

3   *Melody*   28

4   *Dixon*   36

5   *Melody*   43

6   *Chip*   56

7   *Melody*   63

8   *Tessie*   72

9   *Melody*   78

10   *Joe*   84

11   *Melody*   93

12   *Sandra Mae*   102

13   *Melody*   109

14   *Sammy*   115

MELODY JONES

1 Melody

'She stole my pasties.'

'She didn't steal your pasties.'

'She did, Mel. Them new ones with the silver tassles what I had tailormade in New York. I hadn't wore 'em but twice and she was always pickin' 'em up and spinnin' 'em like and they cost me twenty-five bucks.' Her voice was a distant buzzsaw caught on a pine knot.

'Well, I doubt if she stole them.'

'She did too, Mel! She just stole them goddamn pasties right out of the dressin' room, the cunt.'

'She didn't.'

'She *did*. She's always snoopin' around like where'd you get this and how much did you pay for that and twirlin' them silver tassles on them pasties. Twenty-five bucks I give for them pasties and they was all over sewed with these itty-bitty sequins. All by hand they was.' The speed of the saw increased, its whine angling upward.

'She didn't steal them. Brenda's a lush maybe, and she's been known to turn a trick in the john, but she's no thief.'

'She's a THIEF alright. She's a filthy cocksuckin' thief is what she is and she stole them pasties!'

'O.K., honey, so you lost a pair of pasties . . .'

'I didn't *lose* no goddamn pair of pasties goddamn it! That cunt stole my lousy pasties what I give twenty-five bucks for in New York. And you know what? You know what else?'

He didn't know, and so wrapped his head in imaginary cotton to blunt the shrill tilt of her voice.

'Well here's what! Them pasties was made for me by this very fine lady in New York. And you know who she makes pasties and G-strings and gowns and even headdresses for?'

No, he didn't know.

'Lily St. Cyr that's who!' She snuggled back in the chair now, wrapping her bathrobe tightly round her shoulders, arms caressing herself, head tilted upward to show the best of her snub-nosed, slightly bucktoothed profile.

'Really?' he asked, trying to stroke her with the wonder she seemed to require. And then he regretted it, for the saw charged on through the metallic knot, each tooth screaming as it made contact.

'REALLY? Would I lie? I don't tell no lies never. And I aint a thief either like that cocksuckin' cunt. I may not be no lady, but I was brought up right. I don't steal and I don't roll no drunks and I always gives value for money and I aint always showin' up with no bruises on me neither.'

She flashed a glance that he had to recognize as 'knowing', even though her tiny, close-set eyes always seemed to be sending mysterious messages. Or so he had thought at first, before he realized that the squint and the puckered brows were simple near-sightedness.

His thoughts floated off. What time was it? Should he wear the lamé tonight, just in case Tony and Alfie were back from San Juan? They always came to the bar first thing, and that was funny—gay guys coming to a strip club. What the hell was he doing, anyhow! What he was doing, of course, was to run 'the naughtiest strip bar between L.A. and New York', and if he had tried to run a gay bar the police would have put the lid on him long ago—like they did last week with the Inferno and the Sixty-Niner. And it was O.K. He liked the girls—even this one, whose voice sliced through his thoughts again.

'. . . and she done this really great number for Blaze Storm
once what she wore before she went down on that bed with all
the steam comin' out, and it was black chiffon with like about a
thousand black feathers comin' down the back and all around the
floor and a G-string that was all puredee feathers. Do you know
what somethin' like that costs?'

He didn't know.

'THOUSANDS! And when I hit New York again I was
gonna have her do me this tailormade G-string to match them
pasties and I bet you don't know how much that costs.'

'Thousands?'

She snorted, squinted at him in contempt, and fluffed out her
hair. 'Eighty-five bucks. Eighty-five lousy bucks, and I had it
practically ordered and was gonna wear it under one of them
kimona things they sell at Sears. And then that cunt stole the
pasties.'

'She didn't steal your pasties. Brenda doesn't steal. Maybe you
lost them. Maybe somebody else stole them. But Brenda didn't
steal them. If you think somebody stole them here, then I'll give
you twenty-five for another pair.'

Her voice lowered from high to medium whine. 'Oh that'd
be just great, Melody. Gee, you're really O.K. to work for.'

'I know.' Dizzy little broad: she probably left her pasties in a
dressing-room in Syracuse or Rochester. If she ever had them at
all.

'Real swell.'

'Thanks.'

'You know, I don't even mind that.'

'What?' he asked.

'You know—like that little arm.' She slowed, faltered, then
whined on. 'You know, like when I first came here I thought
how can anybody just walk around like that, and then I thought
well why not? Like that takes guts, and besides Melody's a real
gentleman and in fact a saint, and it's always a pleasure to do
business with a gentleman. He pays good and don't never ask
you to do nothin' funny. It makes you feel real safe. Besides—
I'd never known any real fags before—*really* known them.'

She smoothed the pink terry-cloth bathrobe over her breasts,
tucked it snugly beneath the knotted belt, and squinted at

him through strands of coarse, acid-blonde hair. 'Ya know what?'

He didn't know.

'Ya know, she'd make some pasties for that thing too! Like for when you wear that nice sequined suit she could make ya some little pasties to go on that thing. Like she can make 'em to fit anything, and if you was to say I sent ya . . .'

The voice shrilled on, climbed, peaked, and leveled out at a supersonic whine. The fairy lights on the ceiling were all dusty, a little tacky looking. Maybe he should try something with black light, get one of the display boys to do some art nouveau designs in day-glo and then put in black light in that recess that ran around the ceiling. Give the place a new look. Just in the main bar, where you first saw it when you came in. Not in the back room. Nobody noticed the ceiling there anyhow. And maybe he could have some kind of day-glo suit too. There was a loose wire in the hand-mike. He wondered if Brenda had stolen those pasties. She was a lush, and she liked to get it up the ass— or so they said—and he didn't like her doing johns in the john. But he didn't think she was a thief.

If Tony and Alfie were back, they'd have called him by now, unless they just planned to come in and surprise him. They sometimes did things like that. Maybe they'd have some new films of the ballet. When they all went down together last year, they hadn't even left the house for nearly two weeks, and the boys from the ballet were there every day, most of the day, and every night when the performance was over, and they'd taken some great films. It was the highest house in old San Juan, and they could all sun-bathe nude on the roof, with no one to see, and could look down into the dusty garden of the convent next-door, but they rarely saw a nun there. They took some good films on the roof, but the best ones were at night, inside, when the boys came from the ballet, most of them dressed in some kind of drag or near-drag, and then made up dances. It was like dancing for a living just wasn't enough for them—they had to dance all night, too. One night Chico, who had been a Marine and was really too heavy to be a dancer, wore nothing but a turban made from an old red bath towel and ropes and ropes of plastic beads, and did a kind of belly dance that had them all laughing because Chico kept a tough Marine sergeant look on his face all the time. That was the night Marty shut the refrigerator door on his cock. They got that on film, too. But the best night was when all the younger boys came and were feeling really high from the night's performance and improvised a whole ballet to Spanish rock music that was playing on the radio. It wasn't planned or anything, but it was still just like something that had been choreographed and rehearsed. One of them came leaping into the room, stopped, and stood bouncing on his feet while he unzipped an imaginary zipper and stood holding his cock to pee. Then a second one came in and spun about and stood at another imaginary urinal a few feet away and bounced up and down to the same rhythm. The two kept glancing at each other until the second boy finally made a leap that brought them side by side, and they locked their arms around each other and began to make love, but then someone else entered and they broke apart. The audience never really saw anything but the backs of the dancers, hunched before the urinals, pairing and grouping and groping and breaking apart as new dancers entered the room. Then they began to move away, alone or in pairs, until only the first two remained, arms locked round each others' waists, heads tilted to the side in a kiss, jerking each other off. Alfie's camera ran out of film before the performance was over, but that was O.K. because the earlier parts with all the dancers together were really fine. And the next night they had perfect focus on Chico when he did his belly-dance number with all those plastic pearls, and got a good close-up of Marty going to get a beer and then shutting his half-hard cock in the refrigerator door.

'Well, I gotta go eat now.'

'What?'

'I gotta go eat now.'

'O.K.'

'You gonna give me them twenty-five bucks now?'

'Twenty-five?'

'For them goddamn pasties what Brenda stole right off my dressin' room table!'

'Sure, honey.' He heaved himself out of the deep, down-filled silk cushions and walked into the bedroom. When he returned with the money she was standing beside the door, one hand holding the lapels of her bathrobe closed.

'Gee, Mel, you're a real saint, ya know?'

'Yes, I know.'

'But ya gotta be careful with cunts like Brenda around.'

'She's only here another week.'

'Yeah, me too. And when I get to New York I'll get them new pasties and I'll tell this lady you may wanna order somethin'. Just mention my name.'

'Sure.'

'I'll leave her address.'

'Do that.'

'Well, see ya in front of the footlights!' She gave him the gift of a small, tired bump and grind before shutting the door behind her.

Freed of her lancing voice, he realized that the room had grown suffocatingly close. He threw back massive crushed velvet draperies to reveal a small slit of wire-meshed window overlooking the scaling airshaft that joined the Melody Bar and the Liberty Theater. He inched the window upward in its swollen track and was rewarded with a small gust of warm air, sweet-sour with the scent of rotting garbage. He inched the window down again and flipped the air conditioner onto high. The golden fringes of the draperies shuddered to the dull, mechanical hum.

His body slick with sweat, his pajamas seemed to knot and tighten round him, and he slowly unbuttoned the yellow silk top. Jerking his right arm up and down, he succeeded in slipping off the sleeve. His left arm wasn't much help. He could hold the right sleeve just a little with it, but even that wasn't much help. Carefully, gently, Melody Jones drew the tiny left sleeve off the pink swollen stump of his left arm, drew it off slowly and carefully over the useless, bulbous fingertips that protruded from the end of the arm. Then, as if it were a sickly infant and he a doting, protective mother, he nestled the arm against the matted hair on his chest. Cradling the arm in the shaggy hair, he carried it into the bathroom and carefully sprinkled water on it—clear droplets beading the satiny pink flesh.

Then, without a glance at the mirror, he gathered water in the cup of his right hand and held it up to trickle down his face. Eyes squinted shut, he worked up a good lather by revolving a bar of soap slowly in his right hand, then massaged his face until it was covered with a thick white mask of suds. Mascara dissolved and bled into the foam, so that his face became a death's head, with hollow black gouges where the eyes had been. He filled the basin with cold water and lowered his face into it, shaking his head from side to side, cupping water onto the balding crown of his head, while the deformed stump of his left arm hung free, swaying slightly with his motions like an exotic and overripe fruit rocked by ocean breezes.

He shook free of the water, tossing his head in a shower of droplets, and groped for a towel to blot his eyes. Only now did he look directly into the mirror, as the puffy lids lifted to reveal hot tangles of dark brown veins that made his eyes resemble twin planets after the waste of a thirty-year seige. Then he carefully blotted the black crescents suspended beneath his eyes, the towel wrapped snugly round his finger, patting them gently dry. He had once tried to do something about them, had tried to cover them with pancake, had religiously applied skin bleaches, had experimented with mixtures of greasepaint (Cupid Silver and Sand made the best combination, but they separated under the heat of the stage lights). None of it seemed to help, and now he highlighted the dark circles, accenting them with a touch of black greasepaint, outlining his eyes with heavy, dark bands. On the sign in front of the bar that was what the cartoonist had emphasized—the dark eyes, the heavy black brows, the deep, heavy crescents. You had to know how to make your faults into assets; that was part of show-business.

He would shave and make up later. His beard grew so fast that if he shaved even a few hours before showtime, dark stubble had already begun to appear before he went on, and it looked even grubbier under the lights. Later he would shave, bathe his face in astringent, make up his eyes, accent the brows with a dark pencil, and put just a hint of Helena Rubenstein's Perfectly Pink on his cheeks and his lips. But now he arranged his hair, brushing it all forward and then carefully scooping up the long, trailing ends over his left ear, laying them across the top of his bald head, and pasting them down behind his right ear. When it was a little dryer, but still damp, he would give it a heavy coating of hair spray.

Sitting on the toilet, his knees nearly touched the poster of Judy Garland on the opposite wall. Steam from the shower had rippled the paper and streaked the glass. When he sat like this he always thought he must ask Nick to clean all the pictures one day, but he never did. Poor Judy. It had been such a tragic life, and partly because no one had thought to transpose 'Over the Rainbow' into a lower key—at least, not until too late. He was in New York when she died, and he remembered the slowly snaking crowd of housewives and tearful queens and curiosity-seekers inching its way forward to pay its last respects, and how terrible her makeup had looked. As he neared the doorway, someone had turned on a transistor radio, and her own trembling voice had sounded the last dying notes of 'The Man That Got Away'. Melody had felt his own tears floating his mascara, carrying it away in tiny dark rivers of grief. When he got back to Buffalo he and Chip put together a Garland evening and he performed all her favorite songs, wearing his most conservative black tuxedo. Lots of people had said that it was very moving.

Poor Judy. He flushed the toilet, drew up his silken pajama trousers, and shuffled into the sitting room. He heaved his favorite damask chair round until it faced the long, curtained wall. When he drew the curtains back, he winced as an acid light flooded the room from the bar below. Cantilevered out over the runway that sliced down the center of the bar, the two-way mirror gave him a view of the entire room. Only the small back room, beyond the men's john, blurred out at the edge of his vision, but he could see anyone who entered, could size up the newcomers, and could signal Nick down below if he spotted trouble-makers.

Nestled in plump down cushions, he scanned a world of his own invention. Through the greenish haze of the glass, figures moved silently, as though under water, and he never tired of watching the endless play of this sexual aquarium. The straights came—salesmen in ill-fitting dark suits and hillbillies with rooster necks protruding from the collars of two-dollar shirts, and husbands escaping wives with eternal rollers in their hair. These were the drab catfish and scavengers. They helped set off the glints and flourishes of the brightly dressed queens in tight, basket-accenting trousers and fitted shirts of crepe, silk, richly patterned cotton, often opened to the waist, especially if they had tans to display. These were his angel fish and tetras. And the occasional sword-fish, too—the hustlers and would-be hustlers in their universal second-skins of bleached levis and faded, skimpy t-shirts, the tightly bunched muscles of their arms and legs, the firm rounds of their asses, the stiff arrogance of their bullish necks. They could be dangerous, these fish: there often seemed such anger coiled in them, but usually they were still, seeking some backwash, a corner table or the dim recess beside the juke-box, and with feigned indifference allowed the brighter fish to mill about them, accepting the offerings of drinks and compli-ments as their due, brushing off the occasional groping hand, drinking just enough to justify the sale or barter of their bodies. Yes, they could be dangerous, but they usually made no trouble, and they helped promote the sale of drinks, even if they rarely spent any money themselves, and they helped draw in some of the older fags. Most of the sword-fish swam through because Melody had his business cards stuck into the grating of the eleva-tor at the Y.M.C.A. The hustlers were a lot less dangerous than some of the dykes who showed up: piranhas, he thought. They hassled the strippers and occasionally roughed up one of the younger boys—often one of the college kids. Bull dykes they were, and they had no class. Some of the strippers who came through were also lesbians, but they weren't angry about it.

It was still too early for there to be much to see. Joe was there, of course, and there was one customer at the bar—youngish, a spiffy dresser in a well-tailored pin-stripe suit, expensive shirt, and what looked like a Pierre Cardin tie. He might be a lawyer, a dentist, a stockbroker—maybe a successful insurance salesman. He wore a wedding ring and continually glanced upward into the mirror to see if anyone was entering the door of the bar. So he was one of the closet cases not quite ready to go to the steam baths and have himself an honest lay, and not quite ready to go home to the little woman and knock off a legitimate piece of ass, and choosing this place because it was 50-50. His suburban friends might think he had a touch of wildness, but they wouldn't label him queer if they saw him come out of the place, and mean-while he might be lucky enough to rub thighs with some young hotcha or to get his cock sucked in the john before he hurried home to mix his wife's martini and complain about a late appointment. But he wasn't having much luck today.

Joe twisted the caps from several new bottles and dropped them into the pocket of his jacket. He was a hell of a good bartender. He knew the tricks and didn't try to pull any of them on the house. The bar's profits had risen steadily ever since Joe had begun working there. The door suddenly heaved open and Nick came in at a flat-footed run—late again. He'd been there three weeks and had come in late almost every day. Joe needed help, and Nick did his job, but there was nothing special about him. He wasn't even good-looking. It didn't matter, because someday he just wouldn't come in at all, wouldn't come back. Find himself another job, one he liked a little better, and just wouldn't come back—the wandering Greek. But it didn't matter as long as Joe stuck. When Nick first started, Melody thought it might be fun to be balled by him, just because it had been a while since he had any really rough trade. There was a time when he had enjoyed it, had even thought he might write a book about it—about the Hell's Angel who wore lace panties under all that leather and could only come when his tits were bitten, or the sailor who wanted his cock beaten with a ruler, and the truck-driver who begged you to shove a zuccini up his ass while you blew him. But he had had enough of that—maybe too much. He liked it all a little straighter now, and he didn't mind having to pay for it. Hell, he couldn't blame them for needing a little extra incentive. At forty-five he wasn't exactly young except at heart, and he had a paunch that he couldn't disguise once he had his girdle off, and the arm bothered some people. Most never said anything, but he saw them looking, and either it turned them on or it turned them off. There were guys who wanted to be fucked with it, but he had had enough of the kinky stuff. Just a little straight-forward sucking and fucking, that was all he asked. And if he had to pay to get some of the cuter, younger ones, he paid. He could afford it. He didn't mind.

Tricks could come and go, but his real friends really loved him. He knew that. He was always the first to know about new romances and lovers' quarrels, and who had the clap and from whom, and what new talent there was in town. Of course, he did his part too. He always remembered the birthdays—more than two hundred of them, all carefully marked in his calendar, and he didn't just send cards; he made up a little poem to go with each one of them. At Christmas, too. And he sent a letter of congratulations to 'The Hotcha of the Month' with funny remarks about the size of his basket and an invitation to participate in 'The Hotcha of the Year Contest'. There wasn't a contest for hotcha of the year, but maybe someday there would be. Maybe he would close the bar for one night and have a real Hotcha Contest—all the cute ones parading in bathing suits and doing some talent thing.

What mattered was that he was their friend, and it was never too late to listen to their problems. He couldn't hope to count all the nights that the telephone had signalled him awake to listen to some tearful friend in trouble. Half-sleeping, he would cradle the phone on his shoulder and listen. Listening was a great talent. Sometimes, too, he would give advice—as he did the night Buddy's young lover took a whole bottle of aspirin and wrote a suicide note on the bathroom mirror with his lipstick. A couple of times lately he had posted bail for people caught cruising the library men's room. But mainly he just listened, and everyone felt better with someone to talk to. Sometimes he felt that way himself—that it would be nice to have someone to talk to. But it was better to be needed.

Nick was sweeping up. Joe was polishing the bar. The young lawyer was on his second drink now, and glancing at his watch more often. He would soon be off to suburbia, into the grove of tricycles and washing machines. Someone—probably Nick—had started the jukebox. Purple lights winked as a record lifted into the air and arced down onto the turntable. His hair was dry, and he should put on some hairspray now—while it was all still in place.

He was levering himself out of the deep chair with his right arm when the door to the bar flipped open and Sammy Farrell came mincing in. He dropped back to watch. What a first-class prick Sammy was—always parading around with some cute young trick, showing off, putting his hands all over the kid—as if that showed Sammy off as some kind of sex king. Of course, the kids never stayed around, and Sammy wasn't any kind of king—just a tired old queen with a cheap face-lift that hadn't worked. You could still see wrinkles on his wrinkles. He wore expensive clothes that always looked like something a spade might wear on a good Saturday night, and he had a loud mouth and an over-decorated apartment, and he drank too much. Once he had picked up a whole group of hitchhikers—five or six of them, all with backpacks, all turned on with something. He took them back to his place for the night, and when he started that stuff with the hands, they just locked him in a closet for the night, and before they left they carried all the furniture down and put it on the sidewalk. One of the kids, Eddie, ended up spending the rest of the week with Melody, and all he had wanted was a little grass and some food, and Jesus, Melody got a charge out of that story. That prick Sammy had gotten just what he deserved— maybe less.

Queens like Sammy could give the bar a bad reputation. There he was again, as usual, with his hands all over the kid, and the lawyer almost falling off his stool trying to look at them and at his watch and at the door all at the same time. Any minute now, he'd throw a couple of dollars on the bar and run. Sammy just couldn't keep his hands off the kid, and the kid was even nicer looking than what Sammy usually got. Long blond hair, and even from here Melody could tell that it was clean, shiny. He couldn't stand dirty hair, especially long dirty hair, and he couldn't believe how many of these kids just never seemed to wash. He hated having sex with anyone who wasn't personally clean, and he often had to pretend some kind of sex thing to get them into the shower for a little play, while he really just wanted to get the stink off. It turned some people on, maybe, but he just couldn't enjoy sex with someone who wasn't clean.

The kid had a good, strong face, and he wore jeans and a faded plaid shirt that looked clean too. He was a type Melody could go for—the only type that really interested him anymore. That was a problem, because really clean-cut guys like that were often insulted if you offered them money, but that was about all he could offer. Money, or a place to stay for a few days, food, some grass. And he was a good listener. But this type usually wasn't that interested in money, and they probably had friends to talk to.

Sammy couldn't keep his hands off him. He'd go for a leg and the kid would knock his hand away, always looking straight ahead, never saying anything. And Sammy would laugh that high horse-laugh of his, which seemed to drill straight through the mirror, and a minute later he'd try for the leg again, or rub the kid's arm or pinch his cheek. Sammy was the kind that gave people the wrong idea about fags.

The kid lifted Sammy's hand out of his lap and slammed it down on the bar. Sammy heehawed again, and the kid just got up and marched straight out the door. Too bad, he was a cute one—the kind Melody could have gone for. But that showed Sammy. It was a minute before he even looked up to see that the boy had left, and then he just pursed his mouth up and prissed himself around on the bar stool in a way that seemed to be saying 'silly little bitch'. Then he picked his drink up, wandered to the jukebox as though nothing had happened, put in some change and shook his fat ass around in time to the music as he picked out his numbers. He danced his way back to the bar with his tired old ass bouncing, and plopped down beside the lawyer. Melody laughed to himself because he had seen it coming. The young man dropped a wad of dollars onto the bar, said something to Nick, and walked out the door. Melody always said the mirror was better than television—always something new, and no commercials.

What a prick that Sammy was.

Melody jerked out of the chair and drew the curtains to. Then he heaved his pajama trousers into a secure position on his paunch and waddled into the bathroom to spray down the wisps of hair that floated over his bald head. He would call down and get Nick to bring him up a pastrami and a beer. And while he ate he could decide what to wear tonight. The lamé was looking a little tired, but it was O.K. with a pink spot on it. He should phone an electrician about the hand-mike. Twenty-five bucks for a lousy pair of pasties that the dizzy broad had probably left in a dressing room in Syracuse. But it didn't matter. After all, he was her friend, and that sometimes cost money.

2 Brenda

Jesus H. Christ if it aint enough to make you go back to sellin' pantyhose at Macy's all these creeps around here. Those big motherfuckin' needles and $2000 worth of silicone to get these big melons and there's nobody to look at 'em but a bunch of screamin' fags. Jesus do I hate fags. I mean like I don't care what a person does ya know but it ought to be natural. Jesus H. sufferin' Christ! All these fags twitchin' their fannies around like pussy's gone outa style or like they maybe got somethin' better to offer. And me I got to get out there twice a night and on Saturdays three times and shake $2000 tits at guys that aint even seen a tit before unless it was their mother's which was probably anyhow just driedup lemons or maybe grapes. Christ wouldn't it be awful to have a kid like that? Can't you just imagine comin' home and findin' him all dressed up in your best bra and panties? Christ I'd beat his motherfuckin' pansy head in is what I'd do. Even the straights that come in here and there's lots of 'em but even the straights get like uptight. Like I'm a performer see an exotic dancer and I aint no whore but like if some guy really turns on to these tits and really gets all hot and breathin' hard well shit these tits aren't gonna last forever and a girl's gotta live. Six months and I'll need another spritz or two and it may not cost as much on the coast but it's still gonna cost plenty. And then what happens? What happens is someday I wake up and the goddamn things is on my back is where they are. One day all that juice in there just gets up and moves around and there's all that money shot to hell. You gotta think about that. Aint no tits gonna last forever and then what're you gonna do with a couple of water wings on your back? Become a professional swimmer? Ha-ha and hell no and what I say is if some guy gets off on these knockers which are real beauts he can bounce 'em around a while. In this business you gotta put a little away for the old rainy day. And Jesus Christ I'm a woman with natural sex urges. Not like those creeps out there shakin' their fannies around and bumpin' pussies. Somebody ought to give 'em a real fuck some-day but not me honey being as I don't do no charity work. But they can make you feel kinda strange about it not by sayin' any-thing which they mostly don't but just the way they kinda laugh or just don't really look when the old G-string comes down. Sometimes I think I'd like to rub my pussy right in their silly little faces kinda smear it on you know. Jesus but they give me the holy creeps. Somebody's always doin' somebody in the john when I take somebody into the performers john the goddamn private john they're in there like gangbusters laughin' and point-in' like there was somethin' unnatural about it or the first fuck they'd ever seen. Now this guy is really hot and buys me a couple drinks which I didn't want and which is anyhow crazy because they ought to have fizzy water at champagne prices or at least watered coke at whiskey prices which they do in any decent club. But anyway this guy's really diggin' these tits and wants to knock off just a quickie before he leaves and Jesus H. Christ he's got to drive all the way to Rochester and on the other side at that and it's fuckin' rainin' like Noah's Ark out there. And where are we supposed to go to get it off? I sure as hell can't take him back to that twobyfour dressin' room with that nearsighted hillbilly. Tenbuck quickie. That aint bad between shows. So I kinda slip away like I'm gonna go powder my nose and this guy comes slippin' along after and we'd a been in there and outa there in five minutes if he wasn't so goddamn weird. There aint nothin' medically wrong or anything with screwin' somebody on the rag. I read that in Coronet which is always very informative. It's just how many prejudices you got. The Jews were the ones that started it about its bein' unclean. Dirty kikes. So he had to make some racket Mr. Super Clean Prick on account of not wantin' to get it dirty what a weirdo. But I think maybe he really wanted to do it up the ass anyhow and was just makin' an excuse. But ten bucks is ten bucks and anyway there I am bent over the toilet seat with him slippin' it to me and reachin' around to bounce my tits like they was fuckin' beach balls or somethin' and in they come like a whole damn convention of Faggots Anonymous or somethin' laughin' and pointin' like it was the first time they ever seen a real fuck. Jesus and then they practically elect me their patron saint or somethin' and I can't even hear the Hello Dolly music durin' the next show what with them all whistlin' and stompin' their feet and hangin' onto each other and holdin' their little dicks like they're about to go crazy. Jesus I'll be glad to get out of this place. And it's a good thing Rochester give me his ten bucks first because he pulled out of there before I even knew what was happenin' and come all over my leg. Jesus what a fuckin' mess. I think if I was dumb enough to have a kid and he turned out like them fags I'd cut his dick off. But then Christ there's only a week left and I can get off to Detroit big D. Course he pays O.K. Melody one hell of a lot better than the last place but it just gives you the creeps. What them fairies don't appreciate is I had to pay $2000 for these tits and $200 just for that Dolly arrangement with the tapes costin' extra and over a thousand for all them costumes. Christ I got a pair of ankle straps cost over fifty bucks. And all that practisin'. Onetwothree dip and keep your back straight as a poker and always smile and listen to the beat and size up the crowd and don't fall off the goddamn runway and fight with that motherfuckin' zipper on the satin number that's always catchin' on a thread. I guess they think it's all just gettin' up there and takin' your clothes off but it's like Melba says and she used to be one of the best in the business it's like anythin' else if you do it right it's an art and she's the one what give me the word dansoose and taught me how to say it. It's a French word and in France they know what an artist is and how to treat her. When I get the fare saved up maybe in California I just may go over and dance in one of them casinos and get outa these twobit joints where they don't know nothin' about talent. Of course Melody pays good and don't try nothin' fishy on account of bein' a fag too and you wouldn't believe what some of these guys in other places want to make you do. It's O.K. with me about his bein' a fag because he's good to you and really understands somethin' about show business and is kind of an artist himself. But Jesus sweet Christ he's pretty creepy too with that pink arm hangin' there like a big soft cock or somethin'. Even if the rest of it wasn't so fuckin' creepy here that's still enough to give you the fuckin' willies huh. Probably a good thing he's a fag too because what broad in her right mind would go to bed with that. It'd take a hell of a lot of pesos amigo. Just think about wakin' up and findin' that pink thing with the baby fingers lyin' across your face. Jesus! But he's O.K. really 'cause he understands somethin' about artists. Like he knew right away to turn up the Dolly number so's I could at least hear the beat with all them faggot queers whistlin' and stompin'. And I got star billin'. Course who else would have star billin'? Not them two pastyfaced Polack gogo dancers couple of lesbians probably in those tacky bikinis with the curtain fringe sewed on it. And not that nearsighted hillbilly with her tacky Sears negligee and her bunny slippers. Christ! What a drag she is. Always losin' somethin' and crawlin' around the floor squinted up and blamin' everybody for stealin' from her. Some night she's gonna fall off the runway right into all them bottles behind the bar and then am I ever gonna laugh my royal ass off. She is one dipshitty kind of number. And what the fuck kinda name is Mary Louise for a stripper? I mean that aint got any class or any anything but just sounds like a nun. Little Miss Fuck Face. Like right away I know the first rule is you gotta have a name that really sounds good. Jesus can't you see me billed as Martha? Fuck that honey. Like as soon as I got the shots I knew what I was gonna be which was Brenda the Breast. I mean like Brenda itself is kinda classy without bein' dipshitty and Brenda the Breast well you know what's comin' right? Mary Louise? All that's comin' at you then is one tight mean little pussy. And she's got a big mole right down there right where the bush starts and when she slips that G-string down that's the first thing you see.

This motherfuckin' mole. Well if that aint a turnoff. Now she could get that goddamn thing cut out for maybe fifty bucks do somethin' about that mouse hair like dye it red and call herself Flame or Torch or Embers but shit no all she's gonna do is get some twobit pasties to stick on them pathetic little knockers. She aint no dansoose but just another broad that takes her clothes off in public. If some guy grooves on moles he's in luck. Maybe she oughta call herself Mary Mole. Tightassed little hillbilly probably don't even know what her pussy's for. Probably thinks it's where you store your Tampax. Will I be glad to get away from these creeps. There's some big money in Detroit too. But Melody's O.K. At least he's an artist too and can sing the shit out of some of those numbers. It's just that arm gives me the willies. Imagine wakin' up and findin' that thing in your face? Man that's scarier than Vincent Price. I oughta have these roots done but that last bitch cooked my scalp. She musta used lye or somethin' cause it was three weeks ago and I've still got the scabs. Once I get out to the coast though I can maybe find somebody does it for the stars. But they say Jean Harlow's scalp was like rottin' away even before that guy beat her up and killed her. I seen all her movies and she didn't have big tits at all not really just thirtyfours but they sure as hell looked big on account of her personally bein' on the small side and knowin' how to push 'em up. Mine were thirtyeights and didn't look that big. Then forties and then fortytwos'. I think I'll probably stop at fortysix or fortyeight because otherwise you look like some kinda freak and gotta have everything like custommade or it don't fit 'em. They say them guys from General Motors really know how to spend money. They don't sit on them pesos. I aint gonna let them fags bother me tonight. I'm gonna tie little pink bows in my bush and I'm gonna shake it right in their sissie faces. Maybe make'em throw up. These roots are lookin' fuckin' awful is what they're lookin'. I'd put on the gold spray but it costs twofifty a can and looks green the next morning and is motherfuckin' hard to wash out. They oughta have exotic dancin' on TV like and then maybe people wouldn't have so many wrong ideas about it and could see how much of it's really like art. Gypsy Rose Lee got on television but of course didn't take nothin' off. Jesus but I cried when she died. Just went to bed and cried for hours and then went to sleep. I don't know why because I didn't cry like that when my own mother died. These roots really get me you know. So much that I can't even stand to look at 'em. Scabs or no scabs I gotta have somethin' done about them. It's all them little details what make a difference between a stripper and a dansoose you know. Jesus, but I'm gonna shake me some twat out there tonight shake it right in their fairy faces. Here's pussyjuice in your beer!

3 Melody

Naked like that, he could feel his stomach rise and fall, humping the wind as he ran. Ran hard to get there before it closed, crumpling the YOU ARE THE GRAND PRIZE WINNER card in his right hand. As his fist swung forward and back, he watched from the corner of his eye the pink edges of the card, like feathers protruding from the dark hand, flashing, flying. He had a full minute to claim his prize. Sixty seconds. Less now. Maybe his stomach heaving up and down like that really helped —helped clear away the air, making a tunnel through which his body could hurl itself. The clock chimed again—5:29 and thirty seconds—as he reached the door. He pushed against it and it stuck, held fast against the jam, and he heard the second hand slicing onward, a swift arc of wind. His body struggled its weight against the hard mass of the door, and then he looked down to see the small notice chipping away over the handle: PULL. He jerked the door open and flung into the room. Five seconds. Five seconds. Four. Even with more time, even with time prettily wrapped and tied into bright and endless parcels all his own, what would he choose? How could he ever choose?

Would he want the ballet dancers in their sleek tights, their crotches bulging with sweet and secret tastes? Or the squad of West Point cadets in molded uniforms that exaggerated their already firm curves—the narrow hips, the strong but graceful necks that rose lightly downed from the crisp circlets of their collars? Or would he choose the basketball team—not a man under six-foot-five? Maybe he would win again. Maybe he would sooner or later have them all, each of them, one at a time, singly, slowly, savoringly, and in clusters too—in muscular, twisting, writhing groups of two, three, ten, where only to reach out a hand would be to touch bounties of firm male flesh. Maybe if he hurried, even now. There was still a little time. There was still so little time. There was always so little time. With his single good hand he kneaded the little rectangle of cardboard into a sticky mass that clung to his palm.

Some unrecognized sound from the bar below, or perhaps some clatter echoing up through the airshaft, netted him and hauled him from the airless depths of his dream. Only half-awake, he registered with his eyes without really seeing the half-eaten sandwich on the bedside table, the inch of flat, warm beer in the bottom of the glass. He reached for the clock: 9:15. He had only forty-five minutes before he went on for the first show, and yet he couldn't seem to move from the bed. His body was held by fine cords, his throat dry, and there was a black, bitter taste in his mouth. He cupped his right hand before his face and blew into its hollow; it returned him the hot, sour smell of his own breath. He shifted his body slightly, and that seemed to ease a few of the cords. He shifted again, then gave it up and lay back, looking at the cheap cloth cap that perched at the foot of the bed. Mario had left his hat again, was always leaving something. Melody stretched his body until one foot touched the cap, then grasped it in his toes and wagged it from side to side. Dumb kid always forgot something. Just wanted his money and then to get out, but he had the face of a Botticelli angel and a cock that stood at attention as soon as he walked in. How many hours ago was that? The arithmetic escaped him. The phone had waked him, as usual, but he didn't remember the time, and then Mary Louise had come in with some cock-and-bull story about a pair of pasties. Later he had watched Sammy Farrel make an ass of himself, which was nothing new. Well, Mario could just come and get the hat. Melody reached down to grab it, missed, lurched forward, grabbed again, and tossed it across the room. He could just come back and get it. Always said he wasn't coming back and always came back. It wasn't just that he liked the money or even needed it. The kid loved a blow job and moaned and hammered the bed so with his arms and legs before he came that he clearly wasn't just putting up with it for the money. That just kept him from feeling guilty. Sure, it was probably tough on the kid—really wanting to go all the way but feeling too hung-up to do anything, but it was tough one way or another on lots of people, and he wasn't going to pamper the little Dago. Had given that up long ago. Forty minutes to show-time. Chip had already started to warm up the crowd, and the distant, muffled sound of the piano hung on the air like fine gauze. Melody swung his legs off the bed, snapping the remaining cords. He swayed for a moment at the edge of the bed, still dizzy with the long climb out of sleep. The gold lamé tuxedo or the matador outfit? The gold lamé. It still looked good enough under the lights—especially the pink spot. Tony and Alfie would like that. If they were back.

Chip always began to play at 9:30. He never knew exactly when Melody would make his entrance, but he always started playing at 9:30, and Melody was usually down by 10:00. He hunched his body over the keyboard and dropped his long fingers onto it with careless ease, as though he were scarcely aware of what his hands were doing. People still called to each other from one end of the bar to the other, and a drunk was singing something—not what Chip was playing—at one of the tables next to the platform. Chip bobbed his head lower over the keyboard, listening intently to the sounds his hands carressed from the keyboard.

When he played like this, relaxing and letting his body play while his mind lifted and sailed out over the crowd on the wings of the sound, he had no sense of time. Yet by some minute flowering of nerves, he always knew when Melody had entered, and with a trio of quick, bright chords, ended the song he had been playing. Then he heard the faint crackle of the loudspeaker, saw the pink spot flash on, and he held his fingers poised over the keys. As the black curtains first rippled into motion, he ran quickly through the final bars of the chorus, and when they swung open he hammered all the volume he could into the opening measure of 'Yes, Sir, That's My Baby'.

Melody stood at the center of the pink spot, deep within the recess at the far end of the runway, and he seemed to glow and shimmer against the dark draperies. He wore patent-leather pumps, a gold lamé tuxedo, and a ruffled shirt open at the neck. The jacket and shirt had been custom-made to fit the withered left arm, but they were scarcely noticeable from the distance, in the pale delicate bloom of the spotlight. His voice, too, was like some glittering play of light as it skipped along the notes of his theme song, only to be blotted out by the applause that began to gather and swell even before he had reached the end of the number. He bowed deeply, still hugged by the dark recess of the stage, his face a white, smiling mask against the black curtains, his great black clown eyes aloof, remote. He was the professional performer, the concert performer, composed and elegant. Suddenly his mood changed. He swept the microphone cord behind him with one swift and well-practised gesture, stared at the small hand-mike a moment, and flung back his head.

'Welcome, dolls, to the hottest show in town, where big Melody brings you some little melodies and makes you f-e-e-l GOOD!'

Under cover of the whistles and applause, Melody turned and nodded to Chip. The piano player rolled a long chord and raised his hands into the air. When they struck the keys, Melody was skipping out onto the runway and singing.

'Ooooh, little playmate, come out and play with meeee . . .'

Melody gave an occasional twist of his shoulders as he sang, raising his eyebrows first at one and then another of the groups sitting at small tables near the bar. 'Climb up my apple treeee . . .' Good crowd tonight. If the college kids kept packing in, they'd need a bigger place. But there wasn't a location as good as this one—at least not with this kind of rent. And they liked packing in. He winked broadly at the boy who stood awkwardly in front of the jukebox, a beer in his hand. Jail bait. Couldn't be a day over sixteen. And then, on the final notes he turned, the rhythm slowing, carefully enunciating each word, and sauntered to the small, black-curtained stage, whispering into the mike, 'And we'll be jolly friends . . . forever . . . more'.

Yes, it was a good crowd tonight. He mouthed a title to Chip, and before the applause had stopped he began to croon softly, huskily, 'I've told every little star . . .' He moved slowly along the platform and paused at the end, kneeling down to accept the hands that reached out in greeting, to ruffle someone's hair, to take a quick sip of an offered drink without interrupting his song, and he felt his entire body warmed by the lights, by their upturned eyes, by the music—warmed and lifted and transformed. He was a distant, glittering star that rose and shone above them, showering them with its light. He was theirs and they were his. Part of the glow that warmed him was the glow of their love.

He accepted their applause as a gift laid at his feet. Their whistles and bravos were flowers, multicolored and exotic, that he gathered up in his good arm and pressed to his face. Their sweet odors made him dizzy. He swayed for a moment as in a trance, then remembered himself and, with a great flourish of the mike cord, a silent whip with which he commanded attention, he parodied a sideshow barker.

'And now step right up to see the Golly Sisters. Four of the bouncingest boobs and two of the twitchinest twats this side of Erie, P.A. Show 'em you love 'em, dolls!'

The tape dragged a moment, then whirred into sound—a loud, brassy selection of Beatles music—and the two girls appeared from behind the black drapery, their fringes already whirling. Melody stepped back as they advanced, shimmied with them a moment, bowed again and blew kisses to the audience, and left the girls vibrating the planking of the runway.

Upstairs the noise from the bar was only a faint, rhythmic rush of waves against a beach, scarcely related to the frantic motions he watched through the glass. He sat in the damask chair, gently patting his perspiring face with cotton balls moistened in astringent. He had to be careful not to streak his make-up. The lotion was cool and soothing against his hot skin, and its light perfume filled his nostrils. Yes, it was a good house. The boys were elbowing their way up to the bar and Joe on one side of the runway, Nick on the other, were in constant motion. From here they almost seemed part of the act—the male counterparts to the go-go girls who fluttered their fringes along the catwalk. God, how he envied their energy. They came out gyrating those little asses, spinning their tits, and they kept it up without pause for a full thirty minutes—like wind-up Barbie dolls. His own few short numbers had exhausted him, and his flesh seemed dragged into the cushions of the chair by fatigue. But he would be back down there soon giving them his imitation of Streisand and revving them up a little for Brenda's 'Hello Dolly' number. She was different, this one. Most of the strippers who came through —and he knew most of them personally, the girls who worked the Midwest—always seemed a little bored with their work. It was as though taking off their clothes wasn't much different from waiting tables or selling yardgoods—just another job. But this one really loved it—loved shaking those big plastic tits of hers, and really excited herself when she slid down the G-string and worked a finger along her snatch. He had to warn her more than once about trying things with bottles and candles. That was big stuff in other clubs, but here it could get them closed down. She really had to be a nympho—taking guys into the john like that. But the boys all got a big laugh out of it.

Without interrupting their shimmy, the girls began to back along the gangway. Joe reached up and patted the one closest to him on her flying fanny as she moved past. Melody could hardly tell the two apart, but Joe could. Their number was ending. He used his good arm like a lever to angle himself out of the chair, and stood unsteadily for a moment, the floor seeming to tilt beneath him. He took a deep breath, smoothed the lapels of his tuxedo, and thought of that final image of Streisand as Fanny Brice—the pale face, the long, tapered hands. He checked his hair with a few quick pats. He was ready.

The stagelights were out when he positioned himself, and the house lights dim. With his right foot he clicked the floor switch, and a bright spot struck his face. Chip caught the signal and they were into it together: 'Oh, my man I love him so . . .' Melody sang not just with his voice, but with some distant, muffled need, some dim yearning of the heart, long made mute, that rose and swelled into song, and when he reached for the higher notes his voice seemed to carry with it a heavy load of sexual pain. 'All my life is just despair, but I don't care . . .' There was self-pity in it, and fear and hope, but more than any of that a darkly tangled need that took flight out of the dark shadows of the curtained stage, flew along the gangway, and brushed with its chill wings the hearts of many who stood silently listening. The face, with its gouged, blackened eyes, seemed to float on the air like a tragic mask, and for a brief, fragile moment they were embraced, all of them, in the same desperate hunger for love.

The lights darkened again even as the words 'forever more' drifted on the air. Melody paused a moment to blot the sweat and tears from his face with a wadded handkerchief, then kicked on all the switches. The gangway blazed with light—amber, red, yellow—and he raised an imaginary baton over his head before striding forward on the opening notes of 'Before the paraaaade passes by . . .' A rush of sound—laughter, talk, whistles—swept the bar. It was partly excitement, partly embarrassed release from the grief that had so recently locked them together. Bathed in rainbows of light, in the caress of their laughter and love, Melody strutted and pranced along the stage, nodding to the regulars, winking at the hotchas, giving them all the bounty of his smile, his strut, his voice that danced above them with the clear, sweet tones of a bell. There was no more fatigue, no more distant longing, no more fear as he made love to them, stroked them, excited them, protected them with his voice.

Before the strippers came on, while he was still taking deep bows at the end of the runway, he noticed the boy who had been in with Sammy Farrell. He seemed to be alone. And then Alfie was reaching up to take his hand—Tony standing shyly beside him. They were back, then. He had been right about wearing the gold lamé. 'Hello, dolls!' he said. 'You look gorgeous—as usual.' Alfie handed him a rose. He took it, breathed deeply of its scent, and tucked it under the stub of his left arm to blow them a kiss. So they would have a little party upstairs when the bar closed. He had some great new photos to show them. Otherwise, he might have tried to introduce himself to Sammy's friend. But the boy was so young, and he seemed even better-looking at this close range. He certainly wasn't the kind that made it for money —if he went that way at all. It didn't matter. The photos were

terrific, anyhow, and Alfie would love them. He could stretch
out for a while before the big midnight show. Mary Louise
opened that one, and her intro was right on her tape. So he
could rest now, then freshen his make-up before the next show,
and later they would have a party, and he would hear all about
the boys from the ballet, and he could show them the new photos.

4 Dixon

It's not that there's anything about the gay life that I really miss. I'm a little like Huck Finn: I've been there before, and I can live without it. Pretty much. Still, every now and again I get an itch or something. When it first comes on I start noticing the way some guys sprawl at the library tables, shoes off, legs wide apart, and I get kind of warm in the crotch. Usually I just ignore it. If this marriage is going to make it, and I very much want it to make it, then I have to just ignore feelings like that. I don't know how Dee would react if she knew. She's very broad-minded, and she says that Gide's long-suffering virgin bride was really noble, and Lytton Strachey's autobiography is one of her favorite books, and she thinks *Giovanni's Room* is Baldwin's best novel, etc., etc. But she's no Dora and she's no Madame Gide. She's Southern, and that's maybe part of the problem. Girls down there may grow up fast in some ways, but in others they never seem to grow up at all. Dee's mother, for example, thinks homosexuality was made up by authors to sell their books. Dee's hardly that naive, of course. We have a couple of good homosexual friends, graduate students, that we see a lot of, and she calls it 'a very good marriage'. Actually, she's something of a fag hag without knowing it. She seems to have some kind of response to gay people, and they always seem to like her. Maybe it's because she has this tomboyish look, and she's very quick and responsive and always sympathetic, but doesn't come on in any obvious sexual way. That's probably the reason she appeals to me, but we have a good sex life, I think. Maybe she's a little afraid or a little ashamed. She's not very inventive, and she doesn't like to screw if there's any light in the room, for instance, but that may be because she's self-conscious about having very small breasts. I think they're terrific, but I know it bothers her, and she says clothes sometimes don't fit her the way they should.

We have a good sex life, though, and it's not that I feel deprived or really miss anything from the gay life. Christ, can it be sad, and especially sad when you get older and worried all the time about your figure and having to prove something by the number of conquests you can make—or having to pay for it, which must really be degrading. And so lonely. There's nothing lonelier or more pathetic than a tired old fag. It's bad enough for the young ones sometimes, and it can be fuckin' awful for the old ones. It sure as hell isn't the life for me. Still, every now and again I get the old itch, but usually I just ignore it. Occasionally something happens—like when Dee's having her period—but then I never give my real name or promise to see anyone again, and I never get together with anyone on campus. I always go into the city, and even that's risky enough. I don't know how Dee would handle it if she knew, and she's very important to me. Being married and someday having a family really matters to me, not as a cover or anything, the way some people want it, but just for itself. Besides, I couldn't stand to be a desperate old fag.

Still, even when I do get the hots, I really don't need the gay world with all its gossip and viciousness and sulks and feuds and two-week affairs and cute little overdecorated apartments. And I certainly don't need gay bars. They depress me for one thing, and I don't quite know why, because in some ways they're very honest places: people simply announce by going in what they are and what they're after. But when you're in there it sometimes seems like a jungle, with all these predatory beasts stalking

each other, and everything getting more and more frantic as
closing time comes near—the stalking and the avoiding and the
mincing and the groping. I've been turned on by it, but more
often I just have a feeling of the most awful, suffocating kind of
sadness—as though we're all drowning together.

That's no problem here, because there aren't any gay bars. Or
when they do open up, they get closed down almost as fast.
There's just this kind of 50-50 strip bar, and we're here a year
without my even seeing the outside of the place. Almost by
accident one day I find the one steam bath where there's any
action—any really steady action—but I can do without the bars
and that whole screwed-up gay world they represent.

And when I finally do get to this 50-50 place, it's in a really
stupid way. Stupid because the last thing I need is to get involved
with some loud-mouthed, nelly queen—the kind who might
see you at the theater or the movies and come rushing up with a
big 'Darling!' and put his hands all over you right in front of
Dee, God, and everybody. How to explain that one? But today
I'm in town and have this itch on me and Dee's away for a month
anyhow, visiting her parents from Old Virginia, and suddenly
the name pops into my head like the bad penny: Sammy Farrell.
More than a year ago, when a friend from New Orleans learns
we're coming to Buffalo, he sends me the name—someone who
can show me round the gay scene. I of course throw the letter
away, forget the name, and then today for some crazy reason it
pops into my head. He's in the phone book, and yes, he remembers my friend, and he really sounds nice enough—bright, funny,
kind of interesting. So I agree to meet him in front of the Shera-
ton when he gets off work, and we start to walk, and we end up
at the last place I want to be. Well, at least it's 50-50, this place,
and anyone who sees me there might think I'm there for the tits.
Except that there aren't any tits at 6:00—just me and this nelly
queen and some scared closet case. I can't stand people who start
putting their hands all over you in public—like they owned you.
And it doesn't have to be some fag. It can be just an usher in a
theater. It's my Puritan heritage, I guess, but touching seems to
me to be for people who have some kind of real attachment to
each other—unless it's the kind of just sexual thing that goes on
in a steam bath. But least of all do I want this giggling queen

putting her hand on my leg, rubbing my neck, sliding over to grope me in the crotch. Maybe I'd feel differently if he were someone I really went for, but I doubt it. That kind of scene I don't need, and I get out of there really fast. Sammy Farrell. He's the kind who reminds me just how shabby and sad the whole gay scene can be.

So I get out fast, while he's right in the middle of one of those soprano giggles of his. And then there's really nothing to do. It's not like Amsterdam or Paris or Rome or even New Orleans, where you can have an interesting time just walking around and not *doing* anything. First, it's just not too smart to wander around downtown Buffalo, and second there's not really much to see even if you do. So I have a hotdog and end up watching the second half of *Gone with the Wind*, which has been playing constantly in its 20th revival or so ever since we came here a year ago. I've seen it twelve times already—thirteen if you count the time my mother saw it, on the same day I was born. She and Miss Melanie went into labor together, I guess. It's Dee's favorite movie, and she can practically recite it to you word for word. I like it too, but in a different way—as vintage Southern kitsch. Maybe my mother seeing it in labor has something to do with my writing a dissertation on 'Myths of the Confederacy'. So now I've seen it seventeen and a half times, but that's O.K., because my favorite moment is in the second half, when Miss Scarlett throws up her carrots and shakes her fist at the technicolor heavens and says, 'I swear to God I'll never be hungry again'.

I could stay and see the first half, of course, but I'm not up to that kind of heroic sit, and so I'm out on the streets again with nowhere to go. Certainly I don't relish going home to that apartment filled with Salvation Army treasures and no Dee, or listening again to one of those few tired LP's we have. So I just wander and without really intending it I'm back at the Melody Bar, and there's good noise coming out, and I'm inside with a cold beer in time to see the big star do his (or her) Streisand routine.

This guy is really Mr. Super Strange. He has a shrivelled little left arm, a kind of pink flap that sticks out of the doll-sized sleeve of his tuxedo, and it looks even more strange because he's this great hulk of a guy—tall and kind of heavy. But I don't see the arm at first. What I see when I first go in is this great round face that looks like it's floating far away at the end of this kind of runway that comes right down the middle of a horseshoe bar. He's standing against black curtains, and the spotlight is just on his face, which is really weird and a little grotesque—like a big black-and-white mask. His skin's all pasty white, and his eyes are big painted circles, and the face hangs there in the air like some decayed moon. But what a voice. He really sings the hell out of that song, and it sounds a little like Streisand, too, but much, much sadder than she ever sounds. You can tell he's living for this, that all the feeling and love that he's got inside and maybe some of the hurt and the anger is all pouring into it, and the fags go crazy. Even the straights seem to like it, but it's actually a little hard to tell the straights from the gays, especially with the lights so dim. There's something blasted and wasted and still very beautiful about it, and something very sexual. And then he breaks the mood by prancing out onto the runway, with all the lights on bright, singing 'Before the Parade Passes By'. That's when I first see the arm, flapping around in a gold lamé sleeve as he skips down the runway. Christ, that takes nerve. Or maybe it doesn't. Maybe showing off like that is some kind of compensation, a way of letting everyone know it doesn't bother him, that he's really no different from anyone else. No, it still must take some nerve. I don't like this number as much, though. He seems to be sending himself up with it, camping around like Streisand, but he's still good. The voice is clear and strong, and it doesn't seem to have anything to do with this place or his body.

When the bar lights come up again I can see that it's not really a bad place—I mean, not so outrageous as most gay bars. There are some pretty nelly types swishing around, but there isn't the wholesale groping, and a lot of guys, especially those sitting at the bar, seem to be here for the tits. And do they ever get them. First there's this monster called Brenda the Breast. Jesus, she should shoot the agent who gave her that name. But she's got breasts in spades, that's for sure; two great melon tits that look like they'd make her fall over if she tried to walk. She doesn't walk much. Outside of a few dips and turns she mainly gets down to some writhing on the floor, a lot of breast bouncing and a little stick-finger work down under the old G-string. She may not have much talent, but she sure as hell seems to be happy in her work. Not at all like the girls in Soho. I have a good chance to talk to one of them one night, buy her a coffee. She's from Jamaica, and she has to work five or six different clubs a night to make anything like a decent living, and so all night she spends running from one club to another with her 45's in her hand, putting her own records on the phonograph, taking off her clothes, then running backstage to put them on again and grab her records and head to the next place. You can see it when those girls take their clothes off. They're just tired of undressing. Brenda the Breast or Tara the Tit or whoever she is—she's different. She loves it.

It's not that I really want to stay, but there doesn't seem much point in leaving now—not so early, and especially not with Dee away. So I stay, and the crowd's really not too bad, and the second show gets under way with a pretty good little bump-and-grinder named Mary Louise. Then Melody Jones is on again, and I realize that I've probably stayed just to hear him, since I may never get back here again, and I want to see if he's really as good as I think. He is. He does a lot of campy, silly stuff, sort of playing to the groundlings with in-jokes and slightly gay but not too outrageous patter, but it's fine when he sings. I get a better fix on it when he does 'Bye-Bye, Blackbird'. He could have made it bouncy, but he takes it slow and sad instead, and the piano player is right there with him. In fact, the piano player is better on this number than any of the rest. And it comes on haunting and lost and far-away, a little like the feeling I got with 'My Man', only deeper and richer now, because he's not being Streisand or anyone else—just himself. There's none of the brassiness in his voice anymore, but a kind of trembling that suggests tears. It's all completely incongruous, of course—this big ape of a man with this soft, weepy voice. And then suddenly it fits together, makes sense, because he puts the hand mike into a stand and with his good right arm he reaches round and strokes the left one, strokes it and cradles it and croons to it as a mother might croon to a baby. And I feel this kind of flash in the groin, the itch, because it's all innocent and silly theatrics, but it's also infinitely tender and loving and physical. Then I know I have to get out before bouncing Brenda comes back to shatter the mood of this gift I've been given, and I can't bear the applause and whistles that come after, because they threaten it too.

Walking through those pee-smelling streets, looking for a taxi, I think I could even bring Dee there—just as a kind of off-beat night out. But no, what if some guy I've been with at the baths should turn up? Or Sammy Farrell with his creepy-crawly hands? Scratch that one. All the way home, though, I seem to see that mask of a face suspended before me, and I keep wondering what kind of private life someone like that could have—if any at all. Maybe he just works it all out—the need and the love and the sadness, in his music. It's more than most fags have, but it still doesn't seem enough to make a life with.

5 Melody

After the second show Alfie and Tony were waiting for him at the foot of the stairs. Both wore thin white shirts to show off their tans, and through the translucent fabric there was the glint of gold medallions and charms. 'Beautiful!' Melody said. 'You both look really beautiful.' Alfie rewarded him with an exaggerated bear hug and a small, pecking kiss, but Tony hung back as usual with a shy, embarrassed grin on his face. 'Give us a cuddle?' Melody asked. Tony allowed him the briefest embrace, then pulled away.

Yes, they were beautiful, and he was happy to see them, and they were putting up a good front. Yet Melody sensed as he watched them climb the stairs that there had been a quarrel again, and knew that eventually Tony would curl up somewhere and go to sleep and Alfie would want to tell him all about it.

'Fix yourselves a drink, loves, while I go make a pretty face for you. Be back in a flash!'

He always had to clean up a little after the show—sponge off, put on a clean shirt, a little cologne, maybe freshen his makeup. He couldn't bear to think of sitting there in his own sweat. As he searched through the closet for a fresh shirt he thought that Alfie was too temperamental, didn't really understand the boy, or didn't give him enough credit. Before he met Alfie, almost the only life Tony had known was on the Erie barges, and he still seemed to not quite know how to handle this new life of expensive clothes and cars and jet travel and general idleness. He was smart, though—or smart enough. That was no problem, even if Alfie sometimes said the boy was stupid. He wasn't, and he was as loyal to Alfie as anyone had right to hope. He put up with his moods and sulks and kept his drag clothes in order and tended the garden and did most of the cooking and practically sat at Alfie's feet. Yes, Alfie was the queen, and Tony was someone grateful just to sit at his feet, just to be in attendance.

But Alfie had a temper, and he could be insanely jealous. Tony was cute—cute with something of the cocky, rolling walk of a sailor, and he was blonde, blue-eyed, unspoiled by all the luxury around him. Everybody seemed to want him, as though he were some very special, ultimate prize, and while Tony was very faithful, he sometimes seemed not quite to understand the attention other people paid him. If it was a straight, direct pass, Tony just brushed it off—could be almost violent about it—but if it was something more subtle, he seemed inclined to accept it as simple friendship. Maybe the boy was just grateful to get some attention in his own right. At any rate, Melody could remember one dinner party in particular, when Tony as usual was downstairs before Alfie, taking coats and mixing drinks and seeing that the phonograph was neither too loud nor too soft, and keeping an eye on the first fire of the winter—making them all feel cozy and welcome. But then someone new to the crowd, a middle-aged real-estate broker, seemed to take a shine to Tony, got him involved in a conversation, more or less backed him into a corner, and the two were just standing there, the broker coming on very strong and Tony simply being himself—sweet and shy and hardly saying anything at all—when Alfie made his big entrance in a new red chiffon kaftan, and no one noticed him. Usually Tony would have led the applause and the congratulations, but this time Alfie walked into the room without anyone even noticing him, and suddenly his voice shrilled out, 'Where's my drink, bitch?' Tony ran to get one and everyone told Alfie that he looked simply ravishing, gorgeous, breathtaking, and asked yet again why he wouldn't reveal the name of his seam-stress, and then everything seemed fine. Alfie was witty and wicked throughout the evening, full of gossip and funny little bitchy remarks, and Tony sat in proud and loving attendance—the still moon that glowed in the reflection of Alfie's bright, boisterous sun. But everything had only seemed fine, because hours later, when all the guests had left but Melody, Alfie walked up to the boy, who had just stood up from raking to-gether the last of the coals in the fireplace, and drew back a braceleted arm. Alfie struck him so hard that Tony lost his balance and fell back against the mantel, upsetting a vase of roses. Tony signed on a Great Lakes freighter the next day and simply disappeared for three months. Alfie seemed not to mind, but there were no parties then, and he rarely came round to the bar. Then one night, without explanation, they were there to-gether, and the parties and dinner parties and Sunday brunches started again.

Melody loved them both. In fact, Alfie was probably his closest friend, but he couldn't understand his acting that way. He could accept it as a part of Alfie, but he couldn't understand it. He could only think how lucky Alfie was to have someone really love him and need him like that, and someone willing to accept his faults and still stay with him and still love him. Melody thought it would be worth almost anything just to know that kind of love. He had never had it. And what was worse, he had come close enough to that kind of feeling to have some idea of what he had missed. Of course, it was years ago—more than he liked to remember. He was just a boy then, and he had a terrible crush on his tenth-grade English teacher. He realized now that Mr. Browder must have been pretty strange, but then he had seemed like a god. He could quote poetry for hours without stopping and without making a mistake, and he had been to Europe once, and he had a collection of old movies that took up an entire room in the apartment he had in his mother's house. Somehow Melody had begun going to his teacher's apartment on Saturday afternoons rather than to the local movie theater where his friends all went, and Mr. Browder had let him choose the films he wanted to see, and they spent hours just sitting in the dark and watching them. Sometimes Mr. Browder had friends there, but when he didn't he would sit very close to Melody and clasp his knee during exciting moments, and occasionally let his arm fall down from the back of the seat onto his shoulders. When Melody thought of all the old films they had seen together, he remembered the sweet, strong smell of cologne that had always been heavy on the air. One day Mr. Browder had held him by the shoulders and said, 'There is no deformity so terrible as the deformity of the human soul', and Melody would never forget it.

He flicked off the bathroom light and walked back into the bedroom to check himself in the full-length mirror. This shirt was a little too snug in the waist. The buttons pulled and would pull even worse when he sat down. The new pattern was much better. He could tell Louise when he saw her again just to throw the old one away, not to use it again.

Mr. Browder had come in for a good deal of publicity in Erie, Pennsylvania, when one of the students reported that the teacher had come into his bunk on a school field trip and committed 'fellatio'. Melody had had to look the word up, and cried when he thought he would never see his friend again—that there would be no more of their quiet Saturdays, shut away from the world, the two of them together in that dark room watching the silver shadows dance on the screen. He also cried because Mr. Browder had never committed fellatio with him, and now never would, and the boy he had done it to had terrible acne and teeth that seemed to have green fur on them.

But that was a long time ago, and he had other friends now, and he could love them, too, even if in a different way. He smoothed his shirt front down and went out to greet them. Alfie said yes, that it had been a great success, their holiday, and they had taken films this time in the dressing room at the theater—with Chico of course hogging the show dressed in a pink leotard and twirling into almost every shot. They would all see the films together as soon as they were ready—after one of the Sunday brunches.

'And what a new hotcha they've got, Mel. A young Cuban boy just in from Miami, with the most gorgeous ass and eyes that could make you cry—yards and yards of lashes. You know, the kind of eyes you could swim in,' Alfie said.

'Is he staying, then?' Melody asked.

'To be sure, sweetie. He's one of the chorus boys now, but he'll have some solo parts next season when you're there. He's the most divine dancer. He and Tony got on very nicely. V-e-r-y nicely.' Alfie glanced meaningfully and with pursed lips at Tony, who sat on the sofa idly thumbing through *House Beautiful*.

So that was it. Alfie had got a letch for this Cubano, and the Cubano had only been interested in Tony. And that was maybe what Tony needed anyhow—some young, good-looking guy like himself, uncomplicated, without the flashy clothes and drunken brunches that were Alfie's style. But that was silly. He didn't even know this Cubano, and what Tony needed, all anyone needed, was to be loved, and Alfie loved him deeply in his own silly, jealous way. They would talk later, and Melody would maybe try to tell him that.

'You were terrific tonight,' Alfie said, 'especially in the second show. Was it us you were trying to impress or someone else?'

'No one else,' Melody said, and then wondered for a moment if that were true. 'No, you know there isn't anyone. I just love 'em and leave 'em. You ought to know my style by now.'

'Oh, sweetie, that's what they all—absolutely all—say, but someday you're gonna fall just like a brick shithouse caving in, and then watch out! Why, we'll hear the rumble all over town.'

Melody suddenly felt awkward and shy. The thought that he might fall in love seemed so incongruous and unreal, but he was somehow flattered by the suggestion. Still, it wasn't really his style, and it was better not to think too much about things like that.

'Well,' Melody said, 'you certainly got some color. Both of you.'

'Color? *Col*-or? Honey, you should have seen me the first couple of days. I fell asleep sunbathing on the roof, and this ninny just *left* me there, and I got the most unholy sunburn on my ass. I could hardly sit down—let alone do anything that was *fun*. It was miserable. But it was O.K. for the party. Mel, we had the most absolutely divine party—everyone from the ballet, and Ramon and those funny Americans who run the bar, and that hysterical German fag hag who turns up everywhere whether you invite her or not. Cracked crab we had and melon and

champagne and all the most divine food, and Ramon had pro-
mised he'd provide the entertainment. Well, my dear, she positively out*did* herself. We thought he must have forgotten or
something, but about midnight in comes this whole troop of
street boys, like a circus act or something, and they shake hands
and bow and make all this todo like they're about to do some
acrobatic number. And what do they do? They all take off their
clothes and start *doing* each other! Well, my dear, *did* they get
down to business. They were rolling all over the floor and sucking and fucking just like we weren't even *there*, sweetie. And
they just loved it, and I was so sort of dumbfounded and absolutely en-*chanted* that I could hardly *move*, and I didn't even
think to get any film. Next time we go, though, we'll film the
whole thing. It'll be a *classic*. Not one of those children was over
fourteen—I'm absolutely sure of it, but *were* some of them
hung!'

The last customers would be drifting out of the bar now, and
Joe and Nick would be stacking chairs in the bright blue glare
of the neon lights. What a start it always seemed to give people
when they clicked on; it was as though the light itself did them
some terrible violence. Perhaps the shadows just seemed safer.
He liked Alfie's monologues—always liked the way he made
everything seem so dramatic and exciting. Later they would
have a real talk. He could almost feel it coming. He would
maybe try to explain about people needing to love in their own
different ways, and if there was time he'd ask for Alfie's ideas
about re-doing the bar. He always had good ideas about things
like that—even if they were usually a little too expensive. The
hand-mike had to be repaired. It nearly went out on him again
tonight, and it still made that crackling sound whenever he
moved the cord around.

'It really was gorgeous, darling!'

Melody widened his eyes, leered appreciatively, and licked
his lips. 'I could have gotten into that. How many were there?'

'Oh, a dozen—at least. They were squirming around so and
doing so much sucky-fucky you could hardly count them. But
at least a dozen. Maybe even a *baker's* dozen, and they'd come
and then go *right on* doing it. Oh, they were gorgeous. That
Ramon is really too much—the dirty old man!'

'I nearly forgot. I've got some great new photos for you to see—a whole new set from that place in L.A., and we haven't seen a one of them before. All young boys, and all of them hung like horses. Let me show you.'

Melody went into the bedroom, fishing out the small key that he always wore on a fine gold chain round his neck. Alfie had given him the chain years ago—for Christmas. What they all called Melody's Box stood near the bed—a handsome old dome-shaped trunk where he kept most of the pornography—books and photographs and magazines and films. There was no particular reason to lock the trunk, but it seemed to make it all a little more mysterious and exciting. Melody didn't really enjoy pornography himself—or didn't exactly enjoy it in a sexual way. He liked seeing the clean-limbed, well-formed young bodies—straight and firm and whole—and of course looking at them sometimes gave him a hard-on. But he wasn't the kind who would take a bunch of photographs and jerk off looking at them, or need them to get a hard-on before he could have sex with somebody. He couldn't stand that—just as he couldn't stand making it with people who had to use poppers first. No, what he really liked was just simple, gentle sex. But all the boys knew about Melody's Box, and a lot of people came up when the bar closed just to see if there was anything new there. The trunk was nearly full. He had figured it up once—there must be five or six thousand dollars worth of pornography in there. Maybe more. It was certainly the best collection in town. These new pictures—just a set of twelve in black-and-white—had cost $50, and that wasn't a bad price for professional shots like these. Sometimes you paid even more and discovered that the 'new' set was just pictures from sets you already had, and sometimes they were bad copies of things you'd already seen in magazines.

The new photographs were in an envelope at the top of the trunk, and Melody knew Alfie would like them. They were a kind of welcome-home surprise. When he entered the living room with them, Tony was asleep on the sofa and Alfie was dancing with an imaginary partner, grinding his pelvis, sliding his hands up and down his partner's buttocks, pretending to be in an ecstasy very near orgasm. He was a real clown sometimes, and even if he was often so bitchy, he could be very funny. And he was almost always generous with his friends. That was probably why it was easy to overlook all the rest—because at heart, Alfie was really a very generous person, and it was a shame that a lot of people didn't understand him and even though they wouldn't miss one of his parties, they still always talked about him very cattily when he wasn't around.

Alfie stopped dancing and grabbed the manilla envelope from Melody's hand. 'Oh, doll,' he said, as he flipped through the photographs. 'These are dee-*vine*. They're the best yet. Look at that dong, would you? Face like an angel and the cock of a rhino. Aint that delicious, though!'

It pleased Melody to be able to share things like this with his friends, to be able to give them something. It didn't matter what it was—birthday cards or his hotcha letters or the photos and films. It was a good investment when it gave his friends so much pleasure. Also, they knew they could count on him for a lot more—that they could call him absolutely any hour of the day or night and he would be ready to listen, and whenever they came up after the bar there was always plenty to drink or some snacks if they wanted that or dope to smoke. They were always welcome, and they knew it.

'They're O.K., aren't they?' Melody asked. 'The pictures.'

'O.K.? Sweetie, they're fucking gorgeous is what they are. Do you think they're making them better now? I know there wasn't any stick pussy like that around when I was sixteen. I know 'cause I was lookin' for it, baby.'

'Maybe it's improved nutrition.'

'Or orthidonture,' Alfie suggested.

'Or fall-out?'

'Or homogenized milk. Maybe it's hormone shots. Did you ever hear about Sammy's son and the hormone shots?'

'Sammy who?'

'Sammy Farrell, darling—she of the wrinkles.'

'I didn't know he had a son. Is it for real?'

'Well, my dear, that's *her* story, at least. And the story *is* that once upon a time, probably about ninety years ago, when he was no longer young, he was actually married to a female woman, and they had a son—the apple of his father's eye and all that. And Sammy, being a natural-born size-queen, begins to get very concerned about the boy when he's twelve or thirteen, because his little cock just don't seem to *grow*. By then, of course, Sammy's long since left his wife for the old dick-suckin' trail, but he's still checking on the kid, and naturally he's checking on *that*. The boy's growing up and already has a little mini-bush down there, but he still has this positively *infant* cock. So Sammy takes him off to see some quack sexologist who decides there's a hormone imbalance and gives him injections to increase the flow or something, and a couple of months later that thing is big and growing and then bigger and still growing. When it finally stops, it's this real Barnum and Bailey freak-show number, you know? Well, according to Miss Farrell, the kid's been married six times now, still looking for the lucky lady who can take it all. But, darling, you *must* have heard all this before.'

'No, never. Do you think it's true?'

'*True?* Who *knows*, treasure. Miss Farrell has, of course, a notoriously forked tongue.'

'Sammy's a prick.'

'Like father like son, then,' Alfie laughed.

'Well, I just don't like him, and I don't believe half his crazy stories.'

'We all have our faults, my dear.' And then Alfie faltered. 'We all . . . well, yes, really all of us do have little faults our friends must over*look*.'

Melody was sorry if it embarrassed him—saying that about faults. He wished people could forget about his arm, could just go ahead and talk naturally and not worry about offending him. He didn't mind about it. He had always lived with it and it was as natural to him as his good arm. Well, at least he usually didn't think about it so much. He knew it bothered some people—turned them off or made them self-conscious, but it didn't bother him that much. At least, not all the time.

'It's a good thing lover boy's asleep,' Alfie said. 'He'd think we were just dirty old men sitting here and licking our lips over these perfectly sweet photographs and talking about *nothing* but big dicks. Tony's really very straight, you know—which is another way of saying he's ever so slightly feeble-minded. Oh, that child can be so *stupid*.' Alfie stood up, walked to the two-way mirror, and stood staring down into the darkened bar.

'Yes, he can be positively *stupid*!' He combed his fingers through his frosted hair and tossed his head so it fell about his face. 'Either he's feeble-minded *or* he's a very shrewd little number.'

Melody didn't like hearing it, didn't want to hear Alfie say these things about someone who was so faithful and loving. But it was his business to listen; that was what a friend was for.

Alfie turned away from the mirror, put his hands on his hips, and sighed in exasperation. 'Like this Cuban number, you know. That poor little spic is all moon-struck as soon as he sees Tony— can't take his eyes off him, keeps waiting on him, wants to hear all about life on those fucking dirty coal scows like Tony is some pirate who's spent his life sailing the seven seas. And Tony, of course, eats it all up—really thinks this Cubano is interested in what he's *done*, which is for Christ's sake *nothing*, and not just interested in getting into his pants. So one night I go to bed early with this killing headache—Darvon, my dear, and an ice pack and brandy, and nothing seems to phase it—and go to sleep v-e-r-y late and wake up at like 3 or 4 o'clock, and no Tony. He'd been in bed earlier, and now no Tony. So I wait, thinking he's gone to take a pee or something, and he doesn't come back and doesn't come back. And where do I find him? On the roof. On the fucking *roof* with this spic, and he tells me— has the nerve to tell me they want to see the sunrise. Just like on the barges, you know. The fucking ever-loving beautiful sunrise over the sea! Honey, I wasn't born yesterday, and two numbers like that on the roof in the dark under that *soooo* romantic tropical sky are definitely *not* just waiting for the sunrise. Now, either our Tony-boy is v-e-r-y—but *v-e-r-y*—simple and thinks the spic really wants to see the sunrise, or he's the shrewdest little bastard you can imagine and only playing dumb like that. And I've yet to find evidence of any shrewdness!'

'But what . . .' Melody offered. 'Well, what if he really did want to see the sunrise? Maybe he just kind of missed it.'

'*Missed* it? My dear, I've fed and clothed this child for over three years and have been with him almost every night of those years, and he has *never* expressed any interest in seeing the sunrise. Never *ever*. It rises in Buffalo, too, you know. At least, so I'm led to believe.'

'But you know he wouldn't do anything to hurt you. And besides, he couldn't do anything like, you know, have sex with someone with you that close by.'

'My dear, don't kid a kidder. We've all had quickies with the whole *world* close by.'

'I don't think Tony's like that.'

'No, but that spic may be, and our boy's *much* too polite to say, "Unhand me!"'

Melody paused for a moment and then said, 'No, I still can't think Tony would do anything. I mean . . . well, I sometimes think maybe you don't understand that he's . . . well, that he's always trying to do things to *please* you.'

'By spending the night on the roof with this hotcha?'

'Maybe he didn't think of it that way.'

'Maybe he didn't *think*—that's right. And how could he, with that pea-sized brain of his? But oh, my dear, what a positively *luscious* body that brain picks to live in. That, at least, was smart. You know, I still look at it every now and then—like now, when he's sleeping—and go all goosefleshy all over. That has to be one of *the* most gorgeous asses in creation. Not much in the stick-pussy department, maybe, but one hell of a lot of ass and balls. What's a mother to do?'

'But he loves you.'

'Love? I guess, just so far as that little mind can grasp the principle.'

'That means he loves you all he *can*,' Melody suggested.

'And it means that I'm a terrible old tyrant queen for not understanding him more. Right?'

'No,' Melody said. 'No, of course you're not, but maybe you don't always give him enough credit.'

'That's fine for you to say, looking on from the outside, but that boy's just plain stupidity can be such a trial some-times.'

'He means well, though, and that's important.'

'Pretty is as pretty does, treasure. But why should I bother you with these matrimonial tiffs? It must be very boring.'

'No—oh, no,' Melody answered. 'You know I never mind listening. It's what friends are for.'

'Well, but it can't be any party for *you*.' Alfie sat down in the chair facing Melody's and began once more to fan through the pictures. 'You must think I'm pretty lucky,' he said.

'Oh, yes—I *do*.'

'Well, do you want to know something? Every now and again I really envy you—think you're really the lucky one.'

'Me? No. No, you couldn't envy me.'

'I really do, treasure. I really, honestly, truly *do*. I sometimes think it would really be sooo much simpler just to live alone the way you do and take it when you can get it and let it go at that. Love 'em and leave 'em, as you say. Having to nursemaid a child like this one can be such a terrible drag, dear.'

'But he's really such a nice child,' Melody protested.

'Sometimes—when he isn't being too horribly *stupid*. But I'm absolutely not going to bore you with any more of this.' Alfie stood, smoothed out the creases in his trousers, and fluffed his hair. 'I'd better get the infant home and into bed so he'll feel like getting up for the sunrise.'

'Won't you have another drink?'

'No, sweetie, I've got to be fresh in the morning to see the dressmaker. I'm going to have the *most* stunning at-home creation for our little film-showing.'

'What's it like?' Melody asked.

'Ah, no. That would be *telling*. It's going to be a big surprise, but it *does* have something to do with that stunning piece of antique embroidered silk I got in Paris last winter.'

'I'd forgotten it.'

'So had I, and rediscovering it was a perfect *inspiration* for me. You're gonna love it!'

'I know I will. I always do,' Melody said.

'Of course, sweets. That's why I treasure you so. You're always so wonderfully predictable. I mean, you know, so *reliable*. Now help me get sleeping beauty into a vertical position.'

Secretly, Melody felt it was a shame to disturb the boy. He enjoyed just watching Tony sleep—curled up on the sofa with his head pillowed on his arm. He could have just sat there all night watching Tony sleep, his soft breathing, the gentle rise and fall of his chest, seeming to belong to some simpler space than this one. Perhaps, in his dreams, he was again on the water, watching the rising sun strike a path through the darkness. But of course he helped Alfie, and Tony was still half-asleep, cradled by his dream, when he let them out the side door of the bar. His own body seemed awkward, heavy, grotesque, as he dragged it back up the stairs, hauling against the bannister with his right arm. He wondered if anything had happened on the roof, and then he thought that, if it had, it wasn't so terrible. After all, Tony really loved Alfie, and if something happened on the roof it wouldn't have done anything to change that love. Besides, Melody thought what a beautiful picture they would have made —Tony and his Cuban friend, their bodies twined together as the sunrise made a pathway across the sea to them.

6 Chip

The smell I remember best of all. That and the cold, of course.
Daddy buys the house when I'm twelve as the Yankee gentleman's idea of how a Southern gentleman ought to live. Built in
the '20's, though, it's a little more Gatsby than Robert E. Lee.
It sprawls among the wormy magnolias as an obvious latecomer
to the storied banks of the York River—an ugly city cousin who
came to visit and decided to stay. Only later does poor Daddy
learn that it was built as a yacht club for yachts that never
arrived, and maybe that explains the smell—something like
mildewed canvas, that soaks into everything. That I remember—
and of course the cold. Winter winds slice in round all the French
doors facing the river and in the worst months turn the sixty-
foot living room into a cold-storage vault, and I go downstairs
at 6 o'clock every morning to practise regardless of the temperature. My fingers aren't the traditional blue but a kind of lavender,
and I see them stiff and splinted out on the keys like things that
don't belong to me. Eventually I practise with Daddy's old
white kid evening gloves on. There I sit morning after morning
in the bitter cold, with the smell of rotting sailcloth, with an

occasional slice of ivory heaving up off a key with the dampness, with my fingers feeling like sausages inside those kid gloves, practising Chopin and Ravel. Practise and practise and dream of a concert career. Somewhere along in there, I guess, on one of those refrigerated mornings, with my father asleep in I'm never quite sure which of fourteen drafty bedrooms, I begin to get the sense that my life isn't going to fit the standard patterns of achievement and reward.

And it never has quite fit—making me, I guess, a kind of Gentile schlimazl. My father finds this hard to accept—he being Harvard, Porcelian, former captain of the crew, and all things superbly White Anglo-Saxon Protestant. At moments I think my mother, dimly remembered as dark-haired, flashing-eyed, may have been Jewish, and the child taking the religion of the mother, I am therefore a certified and registered and circumcised schlimazl after all. For a time I associate this nimbus of failure with the house itself—thinking its cross-purposes contagious, a kind of cultural-psychological measles which I contract in adolescence. Everything gets the pox—including, of course, my marriage. It all looks so auspicious, too, this youthful conjunction of the fair-haired musician and the daughter of Daddy's college roommate—gilded stockbroker and international sportsman. The simple village church, somewhat impressionistically attributed to a vagabonding Christopher Wren, is the ideal setting for solemnizing this wedding of art and capital; and yet even as I hurry round to the side entrance to await the organ notes that will tell me the bride is rustling her way into the foyer, and as I step to the chancel, turn, and watch the neon smile that lights her along the aisle, I think: measles. I don't normally go in for omens, unless the omens seem to have it in for me. But when we curve into the drive of Hollyhocks (the name's Daddy's choice— made with immaculate lack of irony), the stench of the York River at low tide is upon us, and the omen is hard to ignore. Of course we try, as we move from one lacey table to another on the manicured lawn, greeting guests neither of us knows, neither will see again, accepting leers and handshakes and kisses and dribbling champagne toasts. But it doesn't work. The sun beats down on the slime the tide has left behind, and the miasma rises and the temperature peaks at 100 in the magnolia shade. Bethie feels faint, most of the guests look green, and I throw up. But we're the lucky ones, she and I, for many of the guests will stay overnight—parcelled out among the fourteen mildewed bedrooms. Yes, we're lucky, for I at last find the car where well-wishers have hidden it beneath rotting hay in the old barn, and she manages to get out of mazes of crinoline and lace and into her (according to the local press) 'smart, discrete beige linen travelling suit from Bonwit Teller', and we're off. I, however, have neglected to provide maps, and the Shell station can offer us Arizona, Oregon, or Rhode Island—but neither Virginia nor North Carolina. So I'm conducting a Wagnerian opera for the first time without a score. Come nightfall and sour stomachs and heat-induced headaches and too-long-repressed sexual longings, we have not found the snug little mountain hideaway ('charmingly off the beaten track') where we will spend the first night, and instead have to start checking out the roadside, pre-Holiday Inn motels. They seem to exist largely for truckers, and they feature four single beds per room. We are too acutely embarrassed to explain the necessity of a double bed, too literal to imagine using only one of the four singles and leaving behind a solitary set of bloody, rumpled sheets. And so we drive on and on—the gas gauge needling over to the red of empty, and in desperation settle for Ruthie's Rest. Ruthie toothlessly offers us the magical choice of single beds or a double, with witch-like circlings of her horny hands letting us know that the latter is right by the highway and very noisy. We take it nonetheless, and to the accompaniment of diesel groanings and the arpeggios of gear-shiftings, we pounce on each other on the lumpy, button-sprung mattress, and I discover we've left it too late, the de-virgining. We have read, both of us, too many iambic pentameters about the blushing bride offering her maidenhead. It now seems anachronistic, but we had touching courtship talks, after hours of sweaty foreplay, about saving ourselves for The Day. So now the day is here, or the night of the day, and we have waited too long. Somehow Bethie's cherry has taken stout heart from our romantic self-denial, has grown strong and determined—a shield to her virginity. Uncoordinated thrusting and probing, frantic grinding of hips does not make it yield. Later, more coordinated, more scientific attack is also useless. Bethie finally tries a sharply-filed fingernail, and that too is driven back. After several hours of siege, with dawn filtering through the broken blinds and the diesel chorus growing more luxurious, we abandon the fight. As she drifts to exhausted sleep, my pale warrior murmurs, 'At times like this, I wish I weren't a virgin.'

The walls finally yield, of course—the following afternoon, in a surprise attack in the back seat of the car, parked at a lookout point near Ashville, North Carolina. But the end is already drawing near—foreshadowed in our low-tide, high-cherry beginnings. Before the year is out, Bethie has drifted away to join the anonymous nubile ranks of research assistants at Time-Life, and I'm drifting in the other direction—out and across the Atlantic in search of my career if not my soul, while Daddy continues, I suppose, to play musical bedrooms. It all happens easily enough, without the pretext of embattled confrontation: that much we worked our way through and beyond at Ruthie's Rest. Bethie is now, so the many-transistored circuitry of gossip has it, something of a liberated female, new-style. Whic hmeans, I suppose, that in addition to having graduated to editorial assistant at Columbia University Press, she has progressed in other ways beyond her vestal virgin beginnings. I try to picture her straighthaired, braless, in aviator's glasses, but vertical hold does a quick shimmy. With me it's still all drifting. In Europe, in those early post-marital months, I seem to drift from one covey of whores to another—not just for sex, but in pure admiration of the consistency, the thickness, of their rituals and life styles. In Hamburg I sample the backstreets of the Reeperbahn. On Herbertstrasse the ladies preen, do their nails, gossip, mold their lacquered hair, twitch whips against booted legs, waiting for a customer to tap at their windows. We stroll past, the young men and the old and the occasional married couple, with the lazy casualness of Sunday window shoppers. And the empty windows fascinate me even more than those filled with flesh. I wonder if the owner has gone to the john, or to visit a sick friend, or if she is in her bed-filled cubicle yipping little yips of synthetic ecstasy into a customer's furry ear. I like the look of those rigid, empty chairs—straight-backed to encourage erect posture and utmost protrusion of mammary tissue, and the cushions neatly piled—onetwothree—awaiting the return of delicate pink and perhaps now somewhat irritated but sweetly douched pussies that ask to be nestled in protective down to save them for the next customer. I wander there night after night, and through the antiseptic courtyards of the government-built high-rise whorehouses, where the girls giggle and smooth their mini-skirts and toss their stylish manes of hair beneath the warming infra-red lights and exude all the casual, cozy, nubile innocence of sorority girls waiting for the bus that will bring in studs from the nearest men's college. I love them all, and I love the hard, sleek-bodied girls who work the streets in Paris in Renaults and Peugeots, and the ample meatiness of the whores of Cadiz, backed against their lime-encrusted wall as though waiting for their turn at the well.

I drift among them, occasionally touching, for as long as the money holds out, and then I find work but hardly the career that had seemed, months before, written into the fine print of an Icelandic ticket. There are bad moments—substituting at perilously short notice for the revered and ancient Spanish pianist scheduled to perform Ravel's 'Concerto for the Left Hand' (omens, omens) with the Seville Sinfonia and discovering that the piano that I was assured would be available to replace the practice horror had not arrived. It will come *mañana*, of course, but tonight I must content myself with a tuneless monster, a nightmare of sticking keys and fractured tones and soundless notes and pedals that resound like a woodcutter's ax. And good moments—a more or less permanent job with a young chamber orchestra in Munich, a kind of haven for expatriate Americans, it would seem, but I finally flee the Bockwursts and the Knackwursts and the over-upholstered Germans who make the beer gardens ring with song. Why, I don't know, unless it's the blood of my secretly Jewish mother crying in my dreams.

It occurs to me then how little, really, I know of my own country, and I set off on the westward trek: Luxembourg to the wastes of Iceland, looking like frozen lentil soup as the plane drops down through the mist, and then New York—an assault of indecipherable, electronically amplified, souped-up, projected, shouted, discordant sound that seems to me more foreign even than the nasal liltings of the Spanish or the throaty gutterings of the Germans. And from there to Ithaca, where I work for a weekend in a piano bar, as a replacement, and finally learn to play 'Melancholy Baby'. Then three months in Rochester at an aggressively French restaurant where newly-rich businessmen display their polished, pearlized wives in the candlelight.

And then here, nearly a year ago, to 'the hottest little strip bar between N.Y. and L.A.' By what curious, spastic flutterings of the wings of fate I don't pretend to understand. I see an ad in a newspaper nearly a week old—a copy of the Buffalo *Courier-Express* thrust down between the bus seats in a nest of crusty Kleenex and Mars wrappers: 'Professional pianist; for review bar'. I phone from the Greyhound bus station as soon as I get in, and an hour later I'm 'auditioning', and that night I'm performing, with my suitcase still checked in a locker at the bus station.

One day I'll drift on, I guess. Buffalo doesn't seem exactly the Wild West that I set my sights on, even if it is a long way from Christopher Wren churches and the jockstrap smell of that house in Virginia, and the ample ladies of the Calle de Ramon. But it's alright. I've got a garage apartment with nothing in it that belongs to me—or nothing, at least, that couldn't be packed into two suitcases—and a forty-year-old ex-nun girlfriend who is eager to make up for lost time. You see, I still seem to be the virgin's dream. Perhaps it has something to do with my long sensitive hands. I like the girls who work here, too. It's a little like just sitting still and letting Herbertstrasse walk by you, and the parade changes every three or four weeks.

In a weird kind of way, though, I probably stay on here for El Bosso. Melody Jones. Every now and then he reminds me of some reject from a Japanese horror movie—something that comes up out of the swamp just as the hero is about to bed down with the bottle-blonde heroine, but he's actually an incredibly gentle, generous man, and there's a tremendous quality of need about him. He doesn't come right out and ask for anything, yet it's as though that shrivelled little stump of an arm has a voice all its own that says, 'Feed me. Feed Me.' And he's one of the most talented musicians I've ever worked with. Sure, he camps it up for the fags sometimes, but he understands a piece of music completely, and he works like a son of a bitch to get it right— just to stand up there and make it sound like the easiest thing in the world. But he knows first what makes it work, how each phrase relates to each other phrase and to the piece as a whole. He takes it apart like a clock and sniffs and feels each little spring, checks its tension, gets the taste of the cogs in his mouth, and then puts it all very carefully back together. There's something almost holy in that kind of dedication.

Of course, it's a hell of a long way from Ravel, but Ravel can get along without me. I sometimes feel that Melody couldn't, or that he'd get along a lot worse, and so I stay on and bear witness. Thinking that he needs me is just so much vanity, I guess, but vanity is the least you can take from a world in which you've done so much to stamp out virginity.

7 Melody

He had hardly dared to hope that the boy would accept his invitation, and yet it was easy enough, had always been easy enough, to ask them up for drinks—the lone wolves who drifted round the edge of the bar, and they often accepted—out of boredom or loneliness or curiosity or perhaps a momentary fascination with the idea that he was a star. Many of them only wanted a sympathetic ear. It wasn't hard to start them talking about themselves, and by now he was a master at probing the secret places that told him whether they were gay, whether they were available, whether they wanted money or simply companionship. In his glass tower, the fading bustle of the bar spread beneath him, he was the ballet master, and he led them carefully, gently through the steps of the *pas de deux* that would tell him what he needed to know. Most of them—even if they weren't interested in sex—were flattered by his attentions, his concern, his sympathy for lost loves and broken promises, confusion, hostile parents—and Melody himself was soothed each time as though old, familiar songs piped in his ear. He knew all their stories and he knew, too, how to insinuate himself into them in ways that insured trust and, often, surrender. But if they shrank away from the hand he laid lightly on an arm or shoulder, it didn't matter. There were hustlers enough if he only wanted sex, but if something more came of these early-morning encounters—some physical sealing of the bonds that an hour or two of drinks and confidences had spun—so much the better.

Yet he had, at first, doubted that Dixon would accept his invitation. There was something about the boy so remote from the gay world, and throughout the first evening there had seemed to be tension in his body, as though he were poised for flight. Melody was surprised, then, to see him back again on Saturday night. After the first show Melody watched him through the mirror, saw him brush off occasional advances, and stand wrapped in his solitude as though oblivious to the sexual charades that took place around him. During the second show Melody felt, as he sang, that something in the boy reached out to him, but knew that it was almost certainly his own imagination at work. Yet faces were like that. So many faces moved into and then out of his sight as he performed, and he often chose one to sing to, teasingly, lovingly, and then the face was gone—and it didn't matter, really, because there were always new ones.

He really hadn't expected to see this one again. The boy was, after all, probably some weekend trick that Sammy Farrell had imported—having by now exhausted most of his local chances. So Melody didn't think about the boy after the first night—or didn't realize he had thought about him until the next evening— a crowded, noisy Saturday night, when the face again floated before his eyes. His breath seemed at that moment to catch in his throat, and he heard the slight break in his voice accented by an electronic splutter from the microphone. Then, as he had the night before, he sang for the boy, for the golden face turned upward to him, and his voice became a pair of arms—lithe, muscular, gentle, that reached out to draw the boy to him, to comfort and embrace. It was as though each band of muscle, each constellation of nerves strove together, conspiring to bring forth one simple, effortless sound, and when he sang like this he knew he was good. For the second show the boy occupied the same place at the foot of the bar, and as Melody sang he felt each note issue from his entire body, spinning out of some darkly hidden recess to fling itself, light-bodied, free, upon the air.

After such a performance his body was always gripped by fatigue, as though he had been clutched by a gigantic, bruising fist, and climbing the stairs afterwards was a fierce struggle against gravity. But tonight he didn't leave the stage to hoist his body upward, aching against the bannister, and collapse into the worn, bottom-sprung damask chair. Tonight he felt exhilarated by his efforts, felt the cool rush of blood leave his brain, his skin grow taut and sleek.

So when he descended the brief flight of hollow, unsteady steps at the back of the stage, and as Brenda's first number blared through the loudspeaker system, he didn't turn to seek the solitude of his apartment, but joined the crowd—reaching out to them with this gift of fine, fierce energy.

Alex was there, and they had scarcely spoken for a year. Melody found something arrogant in the soft planes of his pretty face, in the twist of his shoulders that seemed to suggest that he was too good to be touched—as though he were always shrugging off imaginary hands. But now he was genuinely glad to see him again. He laid his hand on Alex's arm in greeting, and Alex smiled up at him, a hint of shyness tucking the corners of his mouth, and Melody wondered suddenly if he hadn't misunderstood him before.

'How's it going, babe?' Melody asked.

'It goes. And so do you. You were super tonight, Mel.'

'Aren't I always?'

'Sure. But not always that super.'

'Keep that up and I'll ask you to marry me. We haven't seen you for a while. Been away?'

'No. Well, sorta. But busy.' Alex glanced to the side—a proud, nervous shift of his eyes—and for the first time Melody noticed the biker who leaned against the bar, his thin, angular body wrapped mummy-tight in black leather. He flipped a quarter with one hand—spinning it into the air, catching it, flipping it upward again with his thumb while his eyes stared blankly ahead.

'That's Bill,' Alex said. 'My friend from Toronto.'

The biker glanced quickly at Alex, then fixed his eyes again on some receding pinpoint of space visible only to himself.

'Well, I'm real happy for you,' Melody said.

'Yeah,' said Alex. 'I mean, I've been in Toronto a lot these days. It's a nice town, you know. Lots more happening than happens here.' He paused, embarrassed, as though to give his friend a chance to join them, and he and Melody watched the acrobatic coin tumble through the air, rise again, and drop silently into the waiting palm.

'Bill's from Toronto,' Alex said.

'Well, that's real nice for you. I'd wondered why we didn't see our little Alex any more.' And he wondered what they did together, these two. He wondered more than he would have imagined possible, now that he had started this shy, trembling creature in the boy. Perhaps, after all, Alex hadn't been arrogant, self-satisfied. Perhaps he'd just been frightened, and Melody had misread the signals. Maybe they could get together when this thing with the biker was over. He saw the coin flash through the air like a polished blade and wondered again what they did together. Probably not much. He knew the biker's type. Probably the guy just got so drunk or so stoned that he could pretend he didn't know what was happening, and then Alex would blow him, or maybe grease himself up and get fucked. Melody felt his own exhilaration drain away, felt his energy leached by sadness, and he jerked his head as though he could shake away the images of Alex's lonely midnight drives to Toronto, his struggles with the coarse, steel-toothed zippers of the biker's leather pants, the murky brown light of rented rooms.

'Well, you guys come up some night after closing, O.K.?'

'Sure,' Alex said. 'Thanks, Melody.'

Melody moved on, swimming slowly against the crowd, away from Alex and his biker friend.

'Ah, the good professor,' he said as he leaned forward to shake hands with the old man who sat at one of the tables near the bar. He wasn't a professor but a retired schoolteacher, and he had sat at the same table every Saturday night since the bar opened. Melody suspected that he played with himself under the table while the girls did their turns. Except for a perpetual shawl of dandruff on his shoulders, the professor always looked dapper in his dark-blue suits, a watch chain slung across a brocaded white waistcoat, his grey hair smoothed into a tight, carefully brilliantined cap.

'How's the service?' Melody asked.

'First-rate, as usual.' The professor nodded toward the bar and raised the half-full martini glass he had nursed since the bar opened. 'Tip-top,' he confirmed.

'Pleased to hear it,' Melody said. 'Always pleased to see you, professor.'

Through the crowd two queens fluttered toward him like exotic waterbirds. Braceleted arms raised from floating chiffon panels and reached out to him.

'Sweetest! Dearest! Treasure!'

The arms circled him, a hand groped his crotch, lips pressed his cheeks in wet, wide-mouthed kisses, and he couldn't resist them. Again and again he had explained that they weren't to come here in drag, that it was fine for after-bar parties, but that he ran a serious business and couldn't take the risk of a bust by the police.

Fou-Fou wobbled on her spike heels, her knees grinding and buckling as she struggled to keep her balance. Her hair was ratted high into the air and had shifted to one side as though it were melting. With her thick, meat-red hands and the coarse whiskers that she shaved until her cheeks were raw, she was a terrible drag. Mimi was a good one—elegant, cool, with long, tapering fingers that were always perfectly manicured and glowed with pearlized lacquer.

'Don't mind her,' Mimi said. 'We're on our way from a dreary party and I couldn't stop her from coming in.' Mimi's voice was sleek, purring. She had gradually raised its tone through a series of exercises she had developed—working with a piano, raising her voice a half-step at a time, drilling for months until she found and held the upper register of her voice and then softening it to a sexy, womanly whisper. She was getting hormones now, and she was talking about having the change.

Fou-Fou, a shoe-salesman by day, tried to imitate Mimi's feminine elegance and succeeded, usually, in looking like a circus clown. While Fou-Fou trembled on spike heels, her arms churning clouds of chiffon around her, Mimi drew close to Melody, laid a hand lightly on his arm, and whispered into his ear: 'You were marvelous tonight, darling. We only caught the last few minutes, but you were marvelous. I'd swear you were in love.'

'Never,' said Melody. 'You know me better than that.'

'We only pretend to know you better than that,' Mimi said, and Melody thought of Alex, whom he hadn't known at all.

'You'll be the first to know, then, when I do fall in love.'

'Flatterer! But if you don't tell me I'll be crushed. Devastated.'

She presented him her most polished society-hostess smile, and Melody found himself admiring again the subtle perfections of her art.

'*Who*,' Fou-Fou croaked out. '*Who* is that monster with the big humps?'

'That one?' Melody asked. 'That, my dears, is a nymphomaniacal bundle that calls herself Brenda the Breast.'

They stood for a moment watching the stage as Brenda drew up first one breast and then the other, licking her fatly erect nipples.

'Well, I think she's disgusting,' Fou-Fou said. 'And those roots, my dear, are a horror!'

'She really isn't very—you know, womanly, is she?' Mimi asked.

'No,' Melody answered. 'But the straights really go for her. She's what's called a hot number.'

'I think she's a big freak,' Fou-Fou said. 'Jugs like that ought to be in a *circus*.' With one braceleted hand she tried to push the shifting mound of her hair into a vertical position.

'I think I'd better take Cinderella home,' Mimi said. She raised a lightly rouged cheek for Melody to kiss. 'Don't forget— I'm to be the first to know when you fall in love! Or would that make me the third? Bye-bye, dear.'

And then they were gone—Mimi gliding with graceful ease, Fifi pitching about like a schooner running full-sail into a typhoon.

Without having consciously sought him, and yet having moved steadily to the end of the bar where the boy stood, Melody saw Sammy's friend. He saw him, stepped round the few people who now separated them, and presented himself.

'Hello,' he said. 'I don't think we've had the pleasure of your company before. At least, not before last night. Welcome to the Melody Bar.'

'Thanks.'

'I don't think I got the name.'

'It's Dixon.'

'And mine's Melody.'

'Yes—I guessed that! But is it your *real* name?'

'No, but I don't think you want to know the real one.'

'Is it so awful?'

'A little dreary, maybe. And a little fey.'

'Maybe someday you'll tell me, and I can judge that for myself.'

'Maybe. Are you enjoying the show?'

'Not this little number. But she really gets into it, doesn't she? I mean, she can't just be acting.'

'No, I think it's safe to say that all that sticky-finger business is for real. She's given us some trouble, too, but she's only got another week. If I can just keep her from fucking in the john . . .'

'That bad?'

'Worse!'

'This just isn't my style, I guess. Strippers fascinate me, and I spent a nice evening with one in London once—just trying to understand how she really *felt* about what she was doing.'

'And how did she feel?'

'Mainly just tired, I think. But that was a different set-up from this one. The girls here have got it made—only two shows a night.'

'This one's packing a month's work into one performance, though.'

'She seems to enjoy her work,' Dixon said.

'She loves it. She's a born exhibitionist.'

'It helps, I guess—if you want to make a career as a stripper. But it's a little too obvious for me. I guess I like it more subtle.'

Melody wondered, then, if he had really come in to see the girls after all. He tested: 'Your friend Sammy doesn't seem to be in tonight.'

'Friend? No, he's no friend, and I sure as hell *hope* he isn't in tonight. Let's call him a former acquaintance, O.K.? A kind of seven-minute wonder.'

'He's a real prick, isn't he?' Melody asked.

'You might say that—unless you can think of something worse.'

'That'll do. He's actually kind of a sad case, Sammy Farrell.'

'All aggressive old queens are sad cases. Most of them would probably be alright if they just didn't come on so strong. Sammy sounded nice enough on the telephone.'

'But on the telephone you couldn't see those hands, right?'

'Or *feel* them either. God, they've got a life of their own, you know?'

'Yes—real little predators.'

'But how do you know about that?' Dixon asked.

'Sammy's famous for it.'

'About Sammy and me, I mean. You weren't in the bar when we came in together. Were you?'

'No, but I have ways of knowing—all very mysterious, you see. Psychic powers. I'm a kind of warlock.'

'Well, you've got magic when you sing.'

'Really? Well, I was good tonight, I guess. You can't always tell how good you are, but you can always tell if you're *very* good.' Then he decided to push it further: 'Maybe you're the one who made the magic.'

'Me? No, I'm hopelessly literal.'

'You may have powers you aren't even aware of.'

'I doubt it,' Dixon countered. 'I doubt it, and yet it would be nice if it were true.'

'Can I offer you a drink?' Melody asked.

'No, I'm fine,' Dixon answered. He gestured to his glass, which still contained an amber inch of liquid.

'That needs freshening up, at least.' Melody caught Joe's eye, nodded toward Dixon, and then leaned against the bar beside him. 'This one's on the house—by way of welcome.'

'Thank you. I feel very welcome.'

Melody studied him closely as they traded scraps of conversation. He saw the glow of soft blonde hairs that lightly downed the boy's cheekbones, the coarser ones that glinted on his chest where his shirt hung loosely open. He watched the hands, strong and beautifully molded, as they reached to draw an ashtray nearer, closed around his drink, or toyed somewhat nervously with a plastic stirrer. He noticed, too, the heavy gold band that Dixon wore on his left hand, wondering if it were some family heirloom, mere decoration, the sign that he had a lover—or if he were indeed married and perhaps straight and beyond his reach. He was a student. He had been in Buffalo for a year. He had not seen Sammy Farrell before yesterday. It was a start, and he would learn the rest in time. It was unlikely that the boy was straight, having come in with Sammy Farrell, and yet perhaps he was. Melody could be sure of only one thing—that something in him ached for this golden boy, ached to explore the planes and textures of his body. He shifted his weight and brought his hip against Dixon's leg. The pressure wasn't returned, but neither was the leg moved away from him.

There was, after all, nothing to be lost, and so Melody brought out the question simply and directly, 'Would you like to join me upstairs for a nightcap?'

'Upstairs?'

'Yes, I've got an apartment over the bar.'

Dixon hesitated a moment and then said, 'Yes, I would.' He turned to face Melody and met the look in his eyes as simply and directly as the question had been asked. 'I'd like that very much.'

A sweet wave of anticipation seemed to bathe Melody's groin, and his cock rose slightly as Dixon's leg pressed timidly but firmly against him.

8 Tessie

I get here 'bout two or three times a year and it's always like takin' a vacation. I've got a real followin' here—ya know? Ya don't see too many twirlers anymore and I'm not just whistlin' Dixie when I say I'm one of the best. It aint somethin' ya can learn neither. It's like a talent ya gotta be born with—like bein' a ballet dancer or a piana player. Them muscles moves or they don't. And then ya gotta work hard—gotta really work at it if ya wanna be a first-class twirler. Comin' here is always like bein' on a vacation—ya know? I got lots of friends here—the regulars—Melody's friends—what really make me feel special. First night they always gimme roses or somethin' on account of how much I like flowers—and that makes a big difference huh? And like I always stay at the Standard Arms every time I come and I get the same room—third floor at the back—away from the traffic—and Jeb and May they both treats me like their own daughter. That makes a difference—ya know? An' I do me a little shoppin' —see. Now I really have me some fun shoppin' at Hengerers— 'cause it's got real class without bein' ya know this kinda snobby snooty place. Real nice merchandise and always good stuff on

sale. Like today I get me this real nice real classy-lookin' kinda
necklace made outa big plastic daisies—and these big plastic
daisy earrings—and not that cheap plastic what ya see most
places but really good stuff—made in Italy. I'm real soft for
flowers—any kinda flowers. Someday when I retire I'm gonna
have a windowbox all full of flowers—all kinds. Retire! That's a
laugh. I got a friend what I see in Chicago and her and me's been
friends nearly ten years almost and I always see her when I plays
Chicago and she says I ain't never gonna retire but am gonna be
twirlin' at my own funeral. Maybe she's right. Whatta way ta
go—huh? Maybe so. Like—twirlin's different from strippin'.
Like if you're stripping ya can maybe go til you're forty-five or
fifty—if ya watch what ya eat an' don't get too saggy—maybe
get a little spritz of plastic ta hold the boobies up. But it don't
make so much difference if you're twirlin'. What really matters
is how good ya are. Most twirlers gets kinda heavy cause of all
that exercise—but that don't matter—'cause there's plenty guys
what likes broads a little heavy. And ya aint just takin' off your
clothes so some guy can look at your tits. You're performin'—
and they're watchin' the action. Anybody can take their clothes
off but twirlin's a gift—like you've got them muscles or you
aint. Me—I got muscles in spades and I knows how to use 'em.
And I don't need to be luggin' around some trunk full of fancy
costumes at a thousand bucks apiece maybe and some crazy
props and wind machines or nothin'—just a coupla G-strings and
these atomic tits is all I need. Melody calls 'em that—says I'm the
girl with the atomic tits. And I oughta be good 'cause I been
twirlin' these atom-bomb numbers for nearly twenty years. First
time was when I run away from home—from this son of a
bitchin, stepfather what wouldn't keep his hands off me—and did
me some twirlin' in a hootchy-kootchy show at the county fair
and me only thirteen then. But I already had me these big tits
and could twirl 'em pretty good. Course I couldn't do round
the world or any of that stuff what's made me famous—but I was
pretty good. It took me a long time to get round the world down
just right. That's the one where the right tit goes over the right
shoulder while the left tit goes under the left arm—and then the
left tit jumps up over yer left shoulder and the right tit goes
under the right arm. It's real important that the rest of ya is dead

sitll when ya do round the world cause that's what's so excitin'
about it—that you're just all still like that with your arms
stretched out and the tits flyin'. For music ya need somethin'
with a good strong drum beat to make it look really good.
Course I can't do that at thirteen—but I can already get 'em
spinnin' in opposite directions. My stepdaddy comes to that
show. Wouldn't ya just know that horny old bastard would
show up ta that show? He don't know I'm there but just comes
in and there I am twirlin'—and don't he just drag me off that
stage and drag me inta his car—which was anyhow just a lousy
old pickup truck—and drag me home and beat the tar outa me.
He is one mean son of a bitch—but it don't matter so much then
'cause then I know I got some real talent what I can always sell
and someday I'll just go away for good—which I do. And I been
beatin' this circuit for nearly twenty years and I reckon I can
keep on for twenty maybe thirty more til I can retire and collect
me some social security. I got good savin's too. I aint like some
of these girls what just throws it all away—makes good money a
coupla years and spends it all on fancy clothes. No—me I travel
real simple and don't buy nothin' much but sometimes some
joolry—'cause I loves joolry but I work steady and saves my
money. I aint no whore neither. Like some guys think girls
what dance like us—strippers and twirlers and exotic dancers and
stuff—is all whores and can just be bought. I've had me some
mighty fine boyfriends—and I guess I'll have me some more—
but no one-night boyfriends for money. And I also aint settlin'
down and fixin' some guy three squares a day and washin' the
pee stains outa his underwear and goin' shoppin' with my hair in
rollers and hot pants and havin' ta ask him for a fiver every time
I want somethin' for myself. No thanks. I like bein' independent
and puttin' together this little nest egg and I like twirlin' 'cause
I'm really good at it. People what really knows about it knows
that—and they knows about it here. Like this is one of the best
spots you can work in this part of the country. Course it don't
look like much—aint no big fancy burly house which are anyhow mostly dead—but the crowd's good and Melody pays good
and is—ya know—a real gentleman. I aint never worked for
nobody what knew better how to treat ya. First time I'm ever
here I get appendicitis the second night and go all doubled up on

the stage and this big-ass ambulance has to come roarin' up from Buffalo General—and he cancels the show and goes with me—sits in the ambulance all the way and like holds my hand and tells me jokes. And I don't know what I got—just think I'm gonna die any minute. And ya know—he stays right there all night—waits out there while I'm in the operatin' room and is sittin' by my bed and holdin' my hand when I wake up. Now that's a real friend—ya know? Like he even offers if I'm hard up for dough to pay my hospital bill—which is only because he don't know me real good yet and don't know I always have a tidy balance in the savin's bank as well as my checkin' account in Poughkeepsie where I know the bank manager personally. Also of course a few travelers checks—naturally none of which I need havin' of course good insurance. But that man is like a mother to me—and when I say mother you're not to take it wrong—'cause I don't mean nothin' about his sex life—which is anyhow his own business I always say—but I just mean that when he loves ya this guy he really cares about ya and really tries to help ya—just like a mother ought to do. I really love that guy. Like even if the money wasn't so good and even if I didn't always get that same back room at the Standard which is nice and quiet always—and even if I didn't like the sale stuff at Hengerers—like I'd still probably come here just for that man because he is really like a mother to me. You don't meet many like him in this business—and this business let me tell ya can be plenty tough too—so ya appreciate it when ya meet somebody like Melody. He's a gentleman—and he's also this really good singer. I'm a professional see and I can always spot another pro like me. He's good enough for TV or movies or for really big time in Las Vegas maybe—except that what he looks like which don't bother me at all would maybe bother some people. But he could make records or be on the radio—that's how good he is except that he ain't got much ambition and is I guess glad enough just to be doin' what he's doin' even if it sometimes seems like a waste with so much good talent. This guy's a pro alright. He's also a prince is what he is—a goddamned prince—and I love him. He knows it too. We're just like that—ya know? So aint nobody happier or more knocked out than me when I see this guy in love with somebody. Like he's all the time sayin'

—and I known him for years—that he aint no sucker for that stuff and aint got time for it and love 'em and leave 'em. That's O.K. for some people maybe and I'm a little like that myself— but this big lug with this big heart—like some people is just made ta be in love and some aint and he's one of the ones that is. So I come in Thursday afternoon after checkin' in at the Standard to run through the new tunes with Chip—and that's somethin' too 'cause most of the girls works with tapes but Melody sees to it I got live music and real classy too. This guy Chip could be playin' Carnegie Hall that's how good he is. So I brings in the new music and there's Melody sorta worryin' around about some guys fixin' the place up and makin' jokes and givin' me this big hug ya know. Not like he aint always friendly cause he's always friendly but he don't come outa that room most days before 9 or 10 at night unless it's a emergency or somethin' and sure don't never hang around that bar unless somethin's up. No—he just sits up there lookin' out through that two-way mirror like a astronaut or somethin'. So he's not only downstairs but jokin' around and singin' to hisself and actin' like he's king of the world or somethin' and I just knows he's in love. After we get through with the hellos and whereyabeens and howsthings and all I just ups and says Melody Jones you done gone and fell in love and he don't say nothin' but just gimme this big wink and I know it's true. He's the type just made to fall in love—ya know? All these years up there in that room like a hermit aint good for him and now he's right in the middle of it all and real happy and like he's just a teenager or somethin' and then I know he's really fell for somebody. I see the kid that night and it aint hard to understand 'bout Melody fallin' for somebody like that 'cause he's one smart kid and real cute too—kinda shy but you can tell from a nice family and all. Onliest thing is I guess he's married and that could spell trouble with a big T and I sure wouldn't want to see Melody get hisself hurt by nobody. He don't need that—'specially after he's come down outa that room after all this time I knowed him—but I don't think this kid would do nothin' to hurt him 'cause he's one fine kid and sure acts sweet on Melody. And he aint like some of the guys what come in here— some of the regulars. They're real nice to me and are ya might say fans of mine—but they're kinda funny too. A little weird and kinda feminine—which is alright but different than this boy Dixon. But some of these guys while being very nice to me you can tell just really want to be looked at all the time and don't have the stuff to settle down and really like think about somebody else instead of theirselves. I just never did see Melody lovin' nobody like that and it was sure gonna take somebody special to get him down outa that room. It all makes ya feel good— almost like it happened to me I'm that happy for the big lug. Him and me's like that. And what a party we have that first night I come to town—the kid and Melody and Chip the piano player up there in the like private apartment with champagne and sandwiches and stuff and you can tell Melody and this kid who is named Dixon is really in love. Makes me so happy I almost cry twice I'm that happy—and old atomic tits she don't cry easy cause in this business when ya cry easy ya spend a lotta time cryin'—and I'm not just whistlin' Dixie neither.

9 Melody

It was as though the world had secretly decided to give them respite. The telephone hardly ever rang, and only once did the side bell signal that some hustler, hard up for money or a bed for the night, stood waiting in the dank alley below. Occasionally friends joined them upstairs after closing, but they never stayed for long, and if they began to dawdle, Tessie fluttered round them and shooed them to the door like an anxious mother hen. And so, in the beginning, they rode with the drift of the days.

But when Dixon had left at noon, Melody became restless—fearing that the boy would never return to him, his heart ticking the seconds until he did, dreading the long space of empty hours before he heard Dixon climb the stairs. So he filled the afternoons with activities—ordering new clothes, supervising the painting of the ceiling in the bar, joking with the electricians who installed the new lighting, calling unnecessary rehearsals with Chip, accompanying Tessie on a shopping spree. Only with Tessie did he speak about Dixon in a way that would reveal even a single ragged edge of the fear that grappled with his love. Perhaps only then did he sense how fierce and ruthless the battle was to be.

But more often he felt, simply, strong in his love, his spirit tautly muscled, yet he knew that the finely tempered armor of his defenses was melting away from him, exposing the soft white flesh of his belly to the sword.

When the last light of the day began to fail and shadows coiled in the corners of his rooms like dusky serpents, fear rose within him to lave his body, and the solitude he had once jealously sought for these early evening hours now seemed a hideous burden. Then, suddenly, where there had been only raw vacancy, there was the sound of footsteps on the stairs, and Melody flung open the door to greet Dixon, and they stood swaying in each other's arms, pressed tightly together as if, between them, they would crush the empty hours that had separated them.

Then Melody stood back, wondering again at the magic of this young man's long, perfect arms, his slender hips, his muscular legs. He reached out to place a hand on his cheek, cupping it in his hand, and said, 'I adore you.' It seemed so much more real than 'I love you', words so many tricks muttered and moaned in a frenzy of love-making, or cried out just before they came. Such words were too cheap for them. In whatever time they had, they must deal in some finer currency. 'I adore you,' Melody repeated. 'I adore you,' Dixon said.

And then perhaps they made love, but as often they merely sat and Melody listened to Dixon's recitation of the day's events much as a mother might hear a child exhuberantly filled with the new facts of a day at school. Listening was an art he had worked hard to perfect, but now he found the listening not just a patiently passive act of witnessing but something active, intriguing, and he yearned for each detail of Dixon's anecdotes about the day's mail, an hour at the library, his struggles with a second-hand vacuum cleaner, the book he was reading. 'Fill me,' Melody's eyes seemed to ask. 'Fill me. Make me whole.'

Dixon went down with him for every show, the two pausing at the final turn in the stairs to embrace with the light, quick, confident promise of more embraces to come. While Melody performed they reached out to each other through the bright curtain of light that fell on the stage to rock together the frail and miraculously tender infant of their new love.

After the last show someone might join them for a drink—

occasionally at the bar, more often in the apartment overhead, where they could sit and watch the action unroll before them like a silent film. They enjoyed these moments, playing at a kind of domestic familiarity, then closing the door behind their guests to find a new and exciting stillness in the room.

But as the nights flickered by and the weeks drew themselves out, Melody became jealous of intrusions on their time together, and by the end of the third week there were no more visitors. When Dixon had first climbed these stairs at his side he had explained—lightly, easily—that his wife was out of town for a month. That had been a Saturday night. Now it was Saturday again—a kind of anniversary of their three weeks of loving, but for Melody it was also a Saturday that brought him that much closer to the day when some mysterious female force would sweep between them. Dixon seemed to catch the trace of Melody's fear, and the bottle of champagne set out for a private celebration stood unnoticed as they closed and locked the door and turned to embrace, grapple, tear each other's clothes away, and sink to the floor to make love more fiercely and more hastily than ever before.

Later, Melody whispered, 'I adore you,' and Dixon, half-asleep, mumbled the single, fading word 'I'. Melody helped him stand and half carried him to the bed, the boy's weight hooked under his arm and cradled against his waist as he kicked aside the clothes they had flung across the room. Dixon sank immediately into sleep, but Melody's head pounded so loudly with his fears and his unspoken jealousies that he felt he would never sleep again.

Dixon stretched and rolled away from him in the bed, revealing the golden curves, the flat, cool planes of his back and shoulders, and Melody's eyes searched their faintly-lit contours as an astronaut might have studied some mysterious, unexplored terrain, glowing beneath him by the light of a distant moon. He reached out to touch Dixon and paused, his hand suspended over the shoulder, pale white flesh furred round the knuckles with wiry black hair, and there came deep within his stomach a dizzying nausea that said he would never reach across those few inches of remaining space, that he would never truly touch this man as he wished to touch him. His hand seemed too grotesque, alien, loathsome. It had betrayed him too often, or perhaps he had betrayed it. His one hand had groped so many crotches, fingers measuring the length of hardening cocks, testing the weight of balls, guiding zippers along their tracks, unhitching the backward puzzles of belts, probing assholes. With this hand he had relieved his own aching, unloved, unlovely body, spraying thick wads of come into the tangled hair of his belly or, legs propped against the headboard of the bed, trying to spray it into his own mouth. It had massaged the tips of black cocks and white ones, circumcised and uncircumcised, to start one clear drop of fluid that his tongue could savor as a promise of the feast that was to come. The hand seemed to him now more deformed, more alien than the boneless pink flap that lay curved like an infant in sleep against his body. Poised above Dixon's shoulder, the hand trembled, and a cry of rage and sorrow rose up in his body, emerging as the whimper of a small, death-trapped animal. Dixon stirred with the sound, reached back over his shoulder and drew Melody's arm around him, nestling it against his chest, drawing him into the still haven of his body. Gradually, steadily, the tension flowed out of Melody, coursing along his skin and draining away, as though Dixon's touch were some kind of balm, an alchemy of flesh that transformed them now into a single, perfect whole—once-separated pieces mated, curve against curve, like parts of a jigsaw puzzle fitted together to reveal unimagined pictures.

And so, bold and self-assured explorers, they traveled together into sleep—into the clear, still chambers where no cobweb of dream could brush them. They would awake to dream, laugh, and make love as they had for three weeks now—going to bed as first light glowed along the edges of the draperies and awakening to the sounds of the street—the bray of horns, fragments of voices scattered high on the air, the clang of metal against metal. If Melody awoke first, fear awoke with him—fear that this would be the last morning, that the boy would this time see him as he was, would smell the stench of corruption in the ruin of his body, would be repulsed by the flap of skin that lay useless beside him, that Dixon would gather himself up and walk out the door never to return. But then he would regain the safe harbor of the boy's body and drift again into sleep.

Yet he knew it would end, that these mornings of sweet balm would be over, that another life would claim Dixon and take him away. He was, after all, married, and this was only an interlude, a moment stolen from time while this mysterious Dee was away. Melody had heard her name now so many times, had felt it whisper so often inside his head that she had grown strangely real to him, someone he had known all his life, and he saw her distinctly with flowing dark hair falling in perfect waves round the pale oval of her face, and the depths of her eyes flashing a warning, asserting ownership, mastery, mystery. Smoothly fitted into the lean, easy grace of her body were puzzle rings and talismans and riddles he could not solve and small, smoothly moving drawers of powders and feathers and tiny polished stones whose uses he could neither understand nor guess. She would return; she would take him away. They spoke of her often, and yet they never spoke of the day she would return to claim Dixon. Had this Dee been another man, Melody thought, he might have done battle, fought to claim Dixon for his own, but how could he battle a magic so foreign to him? One day Dixon would go away, and perhaps then there would be no more gentle hours of awakening to each other; perhaps there would only be occasional afternoons or evenings in which bodies grappled against time, fettered by alibis, and the scent of Dee lurking in some unexpected recess of Dixon's body. Yet even that would be enough, might be enough, had to be enough. If his own body could only make Dixon's child, then Dixon could never completely go away from him—then he could see him turn and wave on the stair—turn, pause, wave, and disappear down the stairs—without the agony rising up to claw in the tender garden of his mind.

Melody rarely had such thoughts when Dixon was beside him. It was only when he had seen the boy pause, turn, and wave to him before bouncing from sight round the curve in the stairs, that he gave himself up to them. When they were together it seemed such a waste, and even when fear seized him, he lost it quickly in the interstices, the explosions of stars that came whenever his body formed itself against the boy's. And so now fear flowed away from him like a giant tide sighing away from the beach—fear and self-loathing and loneliness drawing away to the horizon, and even if they would return again he did not mind, for now he could rest, sprawled on the cool sands of his love. When the tides returned again he would have a plan. Somehow he would preserve what they had found, would perfect it and shape it into a work of art, into a clear and perfect song whose round tones would sound forever. It would happen. He would make it happen. Puzzles. Marquetry. The undreamed green valleys and gentle plains that drifted in uncharted promise before the astronaut's eyes. Water dragging itself in a slow sigh away from the beach, lacquering the sand to mirror brightness. Melody slept.

10 Joe

I'm not even awake yet and already I can tell she wants it. I'm still asleep really but I feel her sliding her ass around and she's still asleep too but I know even asleep what it is she wants. She can't never get enough this woman and that's O.K. with me. They say that's why it's called a piece—'cause nobody ever gets all of it—but I sure am gonna get me as much as I can while I can. It isn't that she says anything or does anything really except that I can feel her ass all big and soft and warm get even warmer and kind of snuggle against me and we're both of us still asleep really but it just kind of moves a little against me not rubbing me but letting me know it's ready and I can feel John Henry getting hard—kind of pushing down into that soft spot where the ass stops being ass and starts being pussy and I guess he wants a piece and you can sure tell she wants it. She moves just a little and her ass kinda hugs me and I snuggle up against it like a big soft pillow and John Henry's a little closer now to the payoff and slides forward to where it starts getting a little damp and it's like he's the only one awake and going out and sniffing for what he wants. And I still don't really wake up good but when she humps her ass back I kinda hump forward and then old John's got his head in there real easy and slow—just the head at first and then shove and he's all the way sliding in there where it's warm and tight and dark and she makes just this one little noise but the same kind of little half noise she makes when she's waking up. It's good like this in the mornings all sweet and slow and easy and without any fuss before you wake up good and she's nice and tight—says she's got a virgin's pussy and maybe it's because she never had kids. It's not that we try not to have them and it might be nice to have one or maybe two but it's been ten years and I guess if the spark was gonna catch it would have caught by now. It's good to really get up there in the old saddle and ride and she calls me cowboy then but it's nice like this too—not awake all the way and real slow in and out like a dream that isn't a dream. And after a while she starts to milk it. I can feel it all moving inside instead of just outside and all along John Henry she's working these tricks like hands in there milking him and so I can tell she's almost ready and then she locks down on it and really pumps it—jerks it off inside her. And then it's over and after a while old John Henry gets a little soft and comes sliding out a little at a time and then all the way out and happy and she pushes her big soft ass up against him to keep him warm and neither one of us really awake even then. It's always good stuff and old John he never seems to get enough of it. Sometimes when we do it like this still asleep we forget about it and wake up and start talking and then one of us remembers about it or we can tell from the sheets and we start talking about it and old John gets ready to go again and we have to do it then. I guess he just wants to see if he can't get all of it but can't nobody get all of it and that's why they call it a piece. I sure aim to get as much of it as I can while the getting's good—and the getting is mighty good, best I ever had and I'm not looking for nothin' else. Good thing too because working in the kind of place I work with snatch shaking in your face every night—old John he wouldn't give me any rest otherwise. But he gets all he wants and don't need no messing around with any of that traveling stuff. Course, it's nice to grab a feel every now and then. Just to keep a hand in as they say. That don't cost nothing and don't hurt anybody but I got me a sweet piece of tail at home and that's enough for me.

I'm not gonna get all of it however much I try and I sure do try.
And then I start really coming awake and I can tell Mary's
asleep and aint no reason to wake her up and I finally reach out
and find my watch. It's always in the same place so I can find it
easy without knocking everything off first and so I find it right
away and it says 12:30 and I think maybe I'll get up and have
something to eat and maybe go out and get a paper but it's a
long time before I stop thinking about it and really do something about it. But I don't go get a paper now because now it's
1:00 and I think I'll get one and read it on the bus to see how the
Bruins did last night—but first I'm hungry. Mary while being a
great fuck is not much in the kitchen and there are all these dishes
in the sink with this kind of yellow gunk all over them. So I clean
up the dishes and scrub down the sink and the counter with Ajax
and wipe off the stove because she'll be glad to see that when she
gets up and a man can really do up a kitchen better than a woman
anyhow and some of the greatest cooks in the world are men.
Then I get me some sardines and saltines and a beer and take
them in and put them on this TV table and turn on the TV and
see the end of this Randolph Scott movie I've anyhow seen
before. Mary likes these really kind of emotional pictures and
sees *Love Story* nine times and cries every time but I don't really
go for that kind of picture. I like westerns. John Wayne is my
favorite western star but I like Randolph Scott too the way he's
all quiet and like a real gentleman until somebody crosses him
and then blam those fists of his are going and you can tell he's
this really tough dude. But he's still this really nice guy. Now it's
a good thing Mary is still asleep so I can open this can of sardines
without her making a fuss because she always makes this face
and says about how they stink up the house. But sardines are
really good for you because they've got all these sea vitamins in
them and they're best of all with some saltines if the saltines are
real crispy to go with the fish which is soft. That's why you
always have to buy saltines that come in individually wrapped
sections just about twenty to a section because then the ones you
don't eat stay crisp and it's worth paying more money so they
stay crisp like that even if the other ones are cheaper. When the
movie's over with old Randolph Scott with his arm around this
sexy little sheep rancher's daughter and the ranch house burning

down to the ground behind them I turn off the set and take this sardine can into the kitchen and very carefully wrap it up real tight in the wax paper that came off the saltines so it doesn't make too much smell in the kitchen and then shove it way down in the garbage can and put the beer bottle under the sink and wash my hands off with a little detergent to get off all the fish smell and go turn me on a bath. I always bathe before going to work even if I don't feel like it because in my work it's real important to be very clean. When you serve the public that's one of the important things—one of the most important things and which I try to tell this new assistant barkeeper Nick who comes in half the time smelling like old socks but he doesn't understand it or doesn't care and he's not ever going to get very far in this kind of business but then he probably doesn't care because for him it's just a job and for me it's a profession and that makes all the difference. Usually the bath running like that wakes Mary up if she's not awake already but she's really sawing logs in there and I guess tired because when I came home last night we had some beers and watched the late-late show even if it was not very interesting. So I run me the basin half full of water and shave while the bathtub is getting full. I always use Noxema Mentholated because with any of the other stuff or even Noxema Regular I break out in spots and then get these bleedy sores when I shave and that's a good way to get skin cancer. I have to be real careful anyhow because I've got a couple of moles and you start cutting them up and you could get cancer too and cancer anywhere on your face or the head can go to the brain just like that —zap! When the tub's full I go get me another beer out of the fridge to drink while I'm soaking in the bath and that's the limit those two beers because any more than that could affect your work and of course I never drink on the job. It'd be real easy to get to be a lush with a job like mine and guys offering you drinks all the time. Nick keeps taking a nip and I sometimes see him finishing up the spiders what people leave behind in their glasses —sometimes a whole drink and that's really dangerous because you never know what kind of disease some guy has and maybe left germs all over the glasses. That's the reason I always insist on really hot water with not only detergent in it but also a few drops of ammonia for washing up at the bar. Like the ammonia not

only kills the germs but it makes the glasses shine—especially if
you be sure to dry them with a very soft and really clean towel.
Now it's things like that that make the difference between a
really professional bartender and someone who just thinks of it
as a job for money. Of course your personality is important too
because it's just like in all those cartoons that I've got stuck up
over the sink at the bar—that people always want to tell bar-
tenders their life stories and sometimes what you hear just makes
you sick or want to cry or to punch some guy in the face like
Randolph Scott but it don't matter you've got to pretend like
you're really interested and smile and be sympathetic and not
let on and try to cheer the guy up if he's really hurting but mainly
you know just try to stay out of the way of trouble but be
friendly too. It's like what they call a bedside manner for doctors
and it's real important in this profession. There's lots of tricks.
Like this business with the bottle tops. Like when you open new
bottles and put in the spiggots you don't just throw the twist-off
caps away or leave them around because that way it's just too
easy for somebody to twist that cap back on and get away with a
bottle. Nick doesn't steal but I've had some guys working with
me that would steal you blind—one college kid clean-cut and
really nice who tried to get out one night at the Plum Inn with a
whole bottle of Old Crow down the front of his pants—walking
like he'd done a load in his britches. No— you keep the fresh
ones locked up and you keep the caps in your pocket until you
can throw them away where it's not too likely anybody's gonna
get out with a not-so-old soldier down the front of his pants.
There's a million little tricks like that. And you've got to be
good at arithmetic too and have like an almost photographic
memory—like if you've got six or eight guys in front of you all
drinking different things at maybe different prices and some
doubles and some singles and some just buying for themselves
and some for themselves and somebody else and you're keeping
an eye on the till and on the traffic coming in the door and whoever's working with you just in case and keeping tabs and keeping the change straight and separate from the tips and all. And at
Melody's especially on a Friday night or Saturday it can be like a
circus with them packed in like that and only us two to serve
everybody and having to collect right away and drinks real

expensive too—being also a cover charge for the show they get
and a real bargain at that. Sure we need somebody else especially
working the tables and Mr. Jones knows it but just try to find
somebody. Do I love a good hot bath. Next to a piece of tail I
guess that's my favorite thing—a real full one where you can
sink back and it comes right up to your chin but without slopping
over the sides and a cold beer with you. A beer sits just right in
this wire soap dish that Mary bought for the tub. I had to bend it
a little so the angle was right but now you can just sit it there and
it's as good as if it was on a table. You can lay back there and feel
that hot water opening up your pores and cleaning them out
and every now and then have a slug of good cold beer. Beer is
very good for keeping the kidneys flushed out and is sometimes
even prescribed by doctors for old people being that healthy.
And a hot bath is good to open up all the pores. You need to
soak for a while like this and it opens up all the pores and cleans
them out and then you rub down real good with a towel afterwards to help close them up again but you still got to be real
careful not to go out too soon if the weather's cold because it
takes a while for the pores to close up. I soak real good and scrub
myself down with some Lifebuoy soap and then rinse the soap
off with this hose thing we got in the tub that you fasten onto the
faucet. Then I get out and rub myself down real good with a
rough towel to close the pores up. I've still got plenty of time
and don't want to go out too soon even though it's not too cold
out so I work on my toenails—but just the big ones. These I cut
every couple of days because if I don't I get ingrowed toenails
which is an occupational hazard of standing on your feet all the
time you're working and even with rubber mats behind the bar.
You got to be careful about things like that or you could really
get all crippled up in the feet. Then I put a little Vitalis on my
hair and massage it good and brush it real hard to stimulate the
scalp—and some Mum under my arms. The spray stuff smells
good but don't hold you against perspiration odor like the
creams do. I brush my teeth and gargle with Lavoris and then I
try to make a bowel movement and this is always a tricky
moment because I am not always regular and because making a
bowel movement for me usually takes quite some time and is a
little noisy so that I like to do it at home and not at work. Today

however I am just fine. Anybody looking on would not guess that I ever have trouble. So then I go to the bedroom to dress and I put on my watch and see that it is after 3:00 and soon will be time to go. Mary is asleep still and doesn't wake up even when I open the closet door which squeaks real loud even after I put Three-in-One Oil on the hinges. She'll be glad to find the kitchen all clean when she wakes up. I have this new kind of clip-on bow tie and have to look in the mirror to put it on. Mary has these pictures stuck all around the corners of the mirror— pictures of her sister and her brother and her mother and her and me on our honeymoon. I don't think this looks very nice putting pictures around a mirror in a home but Mary's family is this very healthy-looking family and has her sister got some beautiful knockers. This new kinda tie is guaranteed to last one entire year or your money back which is a good bit longer than the ones I used to buy in which the springs would break after about six months. Mary is still asleep and I just pull the bedspread up a little to cover her shoulder so that she doesn't get a chill and then its being after 3:00 I leave for work. Now we don't actually open up until 5:00 and I could if this was just a job for me get there at 5:00 or a little before—especially as we don't usually have much clientele before 6:00 with guys coming from their offices and no real clientele until about 9:00 or after. But this is not for me just a job which it is for Nick but is a profession and Mr. Jones pays me a professional wage and so I work in a professional way as Nick will never be able to do. No—I like to be in the bar by 4:00 because that gives me time to be sure everything is in order and the glasses arranged so you can just grab one and not have to even look and plenty of juice in all the bottles and enough beer cold and that's when I place orders which Mr. Jones sees to by telephone the next morning so that you're thinking ahead more than one whole day. There are then always cases to be unloaded and invoices to be checked and you sometimes find mistakes which if you didn't find could cost a lot of money to the business. Also I want to be there early to check on such things like is there enough fresh toilet paper in the johns because this new lady who comes to clean and is very old does not always look for such things. And if the deodorant blocks are almost all gone I put in fresh ones even if there is some left. Every day too I

polish the bar with the same kind of Simonize you use on your
car which gives a much better water-resistant coat than your
ordinary paste waxes. And then at 5:00 I am really ready and if
I am lucky Nick comes sailing in at 5:15 or so always late but can
carry out some cases of empties to the side door where they will
be picked up tomorrow. Now today is to start with just a normal
day because everything looks alright when I go in but something
is a little different maybe. I get a good coat of wax on the bar and
am waiting for it to turn white which it does when it dries and is
ready to be polished. Then I remember that what seems strange
is that Mr. Jones is not already downstairs worrying about
everything looking nice. This has been going on now for over
three weeks or nearly three weeks that every day he is down here
when I am here or he comes down when I come in and has now
all kinds of new ideas about making things look even nicer. He
has these patterns painted on the ceiling by a real artist which
glow in a special light when turned on and looks very classy. He
is also doing measurements about buying new curtains for the
stage to replace the old ones which he says look bad now but I
think look alright and he has lots of other ideas about kind of
fixing the place up and has very good taste about things like
interior decorating which is one aspect Mary is not very good
about. This is all a new turn of events because in the two years
that I am here everything stays the same and I do not even see
him when I come in but only hear him on the intercom telephone
usually when he wants something to eat or drink and then I see
him when everyone sees him when his first show starts because
it is usually Nick or whoever is working with me like Nick who
takes up whatever he wants to eat or drink. I see him then usually
late to talk to him before I go and give him the new orders to
make and of course when he pays me. But lately he is always
down here worrying about things and doing things and having
new ideas and is very friendly and wants to know my troubles
which I tell him are happily few and about Mary and wonders
why she doesn't come in to meet him sometimes. But today he
is not here and while I am polishing the bar with circular motions
I think that this is what is strange about today even though it
would not have been strange a few weeks ago but only normal.
With Mr. Jones there have lately been big changes which I guess

have something to do with this young man who now seems to spend a good deal of time here if not practically live here. I tell Mary of course everything about my work but not this exactly in that she feels already that it is not quite right for me to be working in a bar that has so many of these fairies around. What I tell her is that Mr. Jones respects me as a professional and does not always interfere and lets me do things my way which is the professional way to do them and that such a situation is not always very easy to find. Also the clientele while sometimes a little feminine is very polite to me even though the really feminine ones are not exactly big tippers. And I have a feeling of loyalty to my employer which is part of being a professional—unlike Nick who is simply looking for a job—and I think that while Mr. Jones is a very good singer he does not know much about running a bar and really needs to have someone like me to run it for him who knows all the little tricks and is not going to steal him blind. Also I get two weeks vacation with full pay in August when the bar is closed up and another two weeks in January when it is again closed up and that is very good vacation with full pay and we're closed up every Wednesday night. It is very strange I think his not being down here today although perhaps he is out running errands or something even though he doesn't often go out to do things but telephones for them. I don't know why really but it seems kind of spooky in here today even though it is just like any other day the way it used to be but it now seems quiet and I will be glad when that lousy Nick comes in even with his bad breath and all to have somebody to talk to. Meanwhile I put a quarter into the juke box and make three selections so that it will not be quite so quiet in here and while I am doing that I wonder if he is sitting behind that big mirror looking at me. I am still not used to that although sometimes now I do not think much about it everyone having I guess their little peculiarities and why not.

11 Melody

'Dee comes back on Wednesday.'

The words lodged in his brain like the thin blade of a knife.

'It's the reason I came early today—to tell you she comes back on Wednesday.' Dixon had spoken just these few words as he entered on Monday afternoon, and for a time neither could speak. Silence shrouded the room, and Melody felt his body struggle for breath, wrestling the dull, dead weight of the air.

'Then I suppose I won't be seeing any more of you,' he finally brought out.

'Oh, God, don't be silly,' Dixon said.

'I'm always silly. Didn't you know? I'm a silly old man about everything, and it was silly of me to act as though she wouldn't come back.'

Dixon moved across the room, and Melody seemed to see his smooth stride in slow motion—as though an eternity would never complete that easy movement across space. And then Dixon was holding him, his head against his chest. 'You aren't silly. You're gentle and sentimental and kind, but you aren't silly. And of course we'll see each other.'

'But you'll have to lie for that. You'll have to manufacture excuses and slip away and always worry about being found out.'

'I'll manage that. That's my problem—or will be.'

'No,' Melody said, 'it would be our problem. And it's not the life I wanted for you—for us.'

'Don't make it worse. It's bad enough already. Let's not talk about it or think about it,' Dixon said. 'Let's not spoil the time we have. We'll work it out.'

That night they hadn't even made love. They had simply been still together, gentle and quiet and considerate, and they hadn't spoken of Dee's return again. In Melody's mind the seed of the plan that had germinated there for many days began to seek its final form. Dixon would go away from him, would have to go away. Even ugly and deformed, he might have hoped to compete with another man, but he couldn't compete with the soft and secret places of a woman. They would draw Dixon away, absorb him, transform him in ways Melody couldn't even guess—in ways that he could only fear. Melody would have to give him up, but first he would create something, would create a single, perfect moment that would live in his mind forever. Then Dixon would live in his mind, a golden young god, forever.

During the following day the plan dominated him, unfolding over and over again in his brain like a looped film, but becoming ever richer, denser in color and form as it repeated itself. The plan became more important than Dixon, than the future they would never share; in its beauty, its single, simple perfection, its images flowed across the pale linings of his brain. They nourished him, bore him up, and in their bright flowering they helped him forget his fear—the simple, terrifying knowledge that he could never return to the hustlers, the passing tricks, the hasty trade in public johns—not, that is, without the realization of his plan.

Again and again he rehearsed the words to himself, imagined Dixon's responses, thought of the other who would join them and was jealous of his own thought, then sure again that the choice was the right one. At first he thought he would speak to Dixon at once, as soon as he entered and before either of them had occasion to mention that tonight would be their last night together—or the last, at least, that they would lie fitted closely together in each other's arms, the hours drifting them toward morning, when they would awaken to discover each other again. He was realistic, too, and he knew that on some pretext or other Dixon would come to him again for a stolen night— but he knew that it wouldn't be the same then, and so he needed his plan.

Yet the quick grip of some chill and unseen hand held him back. He didn't speak of it when Dixon arrived. He brought twenty-three red roses with him—one, he said, for each of the nights they had been together plus an extra for the night that was to come. The gift made Melody feel awkward and shy— with nothing visible to offer in exchange, only his wonderful plan. Later, he would explain it. Perhaps between shows. But the first show came and went, and though he sang especially for Dixon, squeezing his love tight and hurling it with each note into the darkness at the end of the bar, he still couldn't speak of it. He would wait. Later, when they were alone after the last show—that would be time enough.

The crowd was good for a Tuesday night—small but appreciative—and he was oddly grateful for that. Tonight they seemed more interested in the girls—especially the Golly Sisters—than in him, but he took their circle of applause as a kind of magic amulet. He was draped in it, protected, secure.

He hadn't told Tessie anything about Dee's returning, but she seemed to understand. Alfie and Tony came in before the second show, celebrating, and insisted that Dixon and Melody join them. It wasn't clear what they were celebrating, but Alfie sulked when Melody stammered an apology. And then Tessie appeared. 'Never mind,' she said, '*I'll* have a drink with you. I'm a lot classier than those two anyhow.'

'Well,' Alfie fluttered, 'we've suddenly gone awfully grand, haven't we?'

'Hell, no,' Tessie said. 'It's just that Mel's gotta balance the books. Aint that right, sweetie? And the kid's gonna help him.'

'That's the latest euphemism, is it? Balance the books? Well, I think it *stinks* when somebody doesn't have time for his own very best friends.'

'I'm sorry,' Melody said, and with his voice he begged for

understanding, pleaded for Alfie not to make a scene, and something in his tone revealed that pain he had struggled to blunt with his plan.

Alfie's voice lost its edge of drunken, bitchy hysteria. 'The queen gives you royal pardon,' he said. 'Come on, Tessie, put those fine tits on the table and we'll drink a toast to them.'

'Damn right,' she said, and Melody turned to look for Dixon. He was no longer standing at his usual place at the end of the bar, and so he must have already gone up to the apartment. As Melody climbed the stairs, the bar, Tessie, Alfie, and Tony, all of it seemed to recede farther and farther away. Now he could tell Dixon of his plan, of this wonderful thing they would make together and cherish—however much or little of life they might ever share together again. It was not so good as making a child, but it would be their own creation.

He swung the door open on the dimly lighted, vacant sitting room. Perhaps Dixon had been in the bar after all, and he was about to descend the stairs again when he heard his name called from the bedroom.

Dixon was there, sprawled naked on the bed, his head propped up by pillows, watching as Melody entered the door.

'I've got another present for you,' he said, 'and I couldn't wait any longer to give it to you.'

As Melody watched him, Dixon's cock began to rise until it stood rigidly thrusting out of the circle of pale, shiny hair at its base. Melody bent over the bed, laid his cheek against Dixon's stomach, and with his right hand tipped the cock until it brushed his lips. Dixon pulled away.

'Oh, no,' he said. 'This is a game for two. You've got to take your clothes off if you want to play.'

He sat up on the bed and helped Melody remove his tuxedo jacket, sliding the small, tightly fitting sleeve off his shrunken left arm, then dragging at the jacket until the right sleeve peeled away wrongside-out, unfurling its scarlet silk lining. With his good hand Melody loosened his tie and began slowly to open the buttons of his shirt. 'I'll do that,' Dixon said. 'I can do it faster.' He paused, then looked into Melody's eyes. 'I didn't *mean* anything by that,' he said, 'except that I can't wait to get at you.' And when Melody didn't reply he said, 'I adore you.'

'Oh, I adore you too,' Melody said, and his eyes brimmed with tears.

Dixon leaned forward to kiss the tears away. 'Come on, now,' he said. 'I'm horny as hell, and if we're not careful, this thing may go off by itself.'

And then it was like the first night again. Melody explored the firm planes of Dixon's body, sought with his lips and his tongue to memorize each detail, as though he could never taste enough, never know enough of this flesh. Together they found new positions, new rhythms, new ways to stroke pleasure into each other's bodies, and they continued almost without pause even after they had both come once, but with a slower, rocking rhythm, as though hoping never to arrive at the end of that journey that carried them through moist green meadows that they were the first travelers to explore.

But the end of the journey came, and they sprawled, breathless, sweating, and too exhausted to talk or to move. Finally Melody stood up, shuffled drunkenly across the room, and returned with a damp, warm towel to sponge Dixon's body.

'If you don't like your present, or if it doesn't fit, you can exchange it,' Dixon said.

'It seemed to fit alright,' Melody answered.

'Oh, God!' Dixon's voice was a sudden, sobbing cry, top-heavy with pain. 'God, I don't want to go away from you!'

'It'll be alright. We'll work it out—I promise. I've even got a plan,' Melody said.

'A plan?'

'Yes.'

'Tell me.'

The words wouldn't come. The carefully rehearsed words that should have now come trooping forth refused to move beyond his throat. 'Let me fix a drink first. Bourbon for you?'

'Please.'

Melody returned wearing an embroidered silk dressing gown, carrying two drinks on a small silver tray. Dixon leaned against the quilted satin headboard of the bed, and Melody sat so that he could face him.

'Cheers,' he said, and they raised their glasses together.

'Now what's this magical plan of yours?' Dixon asked. 'Are

you going to kidnap me or give me some kind of mysterious potion?'

'No, not that. But it's an idea I had about how we could . . . well, make something together that I could always remember. I mean, that *we* could always remember. This perfect thing that wouldn't have any ugliness in it but just be all beauty and like . . . almost like a piece, well, a piece of living sculpture. And perfect.' And then the plan spilled forth—not in the words he had rehearsed, but in new words, other words, words that often seemed not to fit, that stumbled over each other in small, quick, spastic rushes without saying what he had meant to say. He spoke too fast but couldn't stop himself, and he heard his voice raise in pitch as he grew excited about his idea, about its perfection. And then he came to the end and had stopped almost without realizing it, for his mind raced ahead, seeking new words, new combinations of sounds to describe this thing they would make together.

And then he heard Dixon speaking and the tower of words building in his own mind tumbled down around him. 'You're joking, I hope.' His voice had the brittle precision of ice.

Melody couldn't answer. Joking? God, no! It was his plan—his perfect plan.

'You can't be serious,' Dixon said.

'Joking?' Melody asked. 'Joking?'

'I hope so.'

'Joking?'

'You sound like an echo. And if you're really, as you say, joking-joking-joking, it isn't a very funny joke. Or maybe I don't have the punch-line yet.'

Melody shook his head slowly, as though even so little motion would shake from his mind the layer of anger that Dixon's voice carried. He had explained it badly. He would try again.

'This guy is special,' he said. 'Not special like you. No one's special like you. But he's good-looking, and he's clean, and he has a perfect body—a really beautiful body.'

'Are you the local dating service?'

'That's not what I mean. I mean just . . . well, just that you're both so good-looking and it would be so classic and perfect . . . like the Greek myths . . . sculpture or a painting.'

'Do you know what you're asking me to do?'

'Not what you think. Not what you mean. You make it sound so . . . make it sound all . . . wrong when you talk about it like that, when you say it like that. You don't understand what I mean. It's just that you're so beautiful and so . . . perfect, and the other guy's not beautiful, but he's good-looking—really handsome, and it'll be . . . it'll be . . . be like two young gods. Not just some sex thing. Not really a sex thing at all—just this . . . just this perfection. It'll be this perfect thing I can always remember, always have. It won't be me doing it, but you can imagine it's me because really it *will* be me only through this other person, you know, and I can watch and imagine it's me, too, and it'll be perfect . . . a work of art.'

'You really are serious, aren't you? You're not joking,' Dixon said. 'Now I'm the one who sounds like an echo, but I don't believe this is really happening. Not to us. Not on our last night together.'

Melody felt the silk dressing gown pasted by sweat to his body. He struggled to understand what was happening, why his perfect plan was failing him—why he couldn't make Dixon see that they could create this perfect thing together and carry it away in their minds and always have it there, whatever else happened.

'He's nobody special to me, if that's what you think. Nobody special. He's just another hustler except that he's so good-looking, and he's hung like a horse, and he's built a lot like you with this really perfect body. The two of you together . . . it could be just like some scene from the Greek gods. And it doesn't matter when . . . when we do it. We could do it some afternoon. You wouldn't have to worry about getting away at night. We could do it during the daytime.'

Slow, softened, but coiled in anger, Dixon's voice rose from his throat in three clipped words: 'You disgust me.'

'Sure I do! I know I do! I knew all along I must disgust you. I disgust me, too!' He seized the stump of his left arm and shoved it against Dixon's face. 'Of course I'm disgusting.'

'Stop it! I didn't mean that. It's the idea of my being with someone else, of your wanting me to have sex with someone else while you watch—that's what disgusts me!'

'But that's what you don't understand. This person doesn't

matter. He only does it for money anyhow. It won't even be him. It'll really be *me*. Don't you see that? It'll be these two perfect people, only one will be me.'

'No!'

'But it'll be so beautiful, and it'll be just like it was me. I'll even hide. I could even hide so you couldn't see me watching you.'

'No!' Dixon shouted again, and his voice was a sob that tore the air.

'Please,' Melody entreated. 'Please, baby. For me, for you, for us, please.'

'You and I were beautiful. We were just together you and I and that was beautiful. So beautiful. Didn't you *know* that?'

'But this is something different. This would be like a work of art that we made together, and we'll always have it. It can be always with us, this thing we can make . . . this work of art.'

'You're crazy. You're sick! Christ, I don't know what you are, but I don't want to know.'

'Don't say that.' Melody pleaded, moaned, 'Oh, don't say that. I'll do anything for you. I'll do whatever you want. I'll buy you something nice.'

'You'll buy me something?' Dixon repeated.

'Yes! Sure!' He took it up, raced ahead. 'Of course I will. I'll buy you something really nice—some nice thing you've always wanted and couldn't afford.'

'Freak!' Dixon's word seemed to travel with his hand as he struck Melody on the face—word and hand together striking, resounding in his mind, darting their pain through his body. Dixon struck again and again as he screamed the word again, first with his palm and then with the back of his hand. 'Freak! Freak! Freak! Freak!'

Melody did nothing to defend himself. His mind grew numb as it wandered, drifted, lost in its search for that point at which his plan had gone wrong. Why couldn't Dixon see? What had gone wrong? And then, dazed, he sat at the edge of the bed, scarcely hearing the sounds of Dixon's hasty dressing, hardly even registering the sound of the door to the stairway opening and briskly closing. Dixon would see. The boy was smart. He would see, understand. He would come back tomorrow, would find some way to come back tomorrow, or would still come back tonight. He would come back or he would phone, and there would be a way to explain it to him. He was sure of that. He would have another chance. And yet as he thought of it, his shoulders began to rise and fall in uncontrollable spasms even before the loud sobbing tore from his throat to rebound in its deafening anguish from the walls of the room.

12 Sandra Mae

We're both still real excited about making our break in show business, you know. I don't think either one of us ever really thought about a show-business career except maybe I did a little when I was taking tap lessons and our whole class did 'South of the Border' on 'Your Town Talent Show' on TV. That was really super, but it was when I was just little. I'd always thought I wanted to be maybe a kindergarten teacher or a missionary's wife and Becky Gae she just thought she'd get married and then be an Avon lady to make some extra money so she could buy nice clothes without having to ask her husband to give her the money. Besides, if you're an Avon lady you're the first one to know when they make some more of those real cute bottles they make. So what happened was that I was going to nursing school and Becky Gae she was selling goldfish and parakeets and things like that at Woolworth's which she didn't like very much. I also didn't like very much being a nurse or rather a nurse's aid which I was going to be because the idea of emptying all those stinky bedpans and cleaning throw-up off people just made me go all squeamy inside. Besides, it wasn't at all like 'Dr. Kildare' or 'General Hospital' which I used to never ever miss because most of the doctors were old and married and there was this terrible smell which gave me a headache something awful. So one night Becky Gae is staying over at my place when my folks have gone to see these friends they go fishing with sometimes who live down near Columbus and I remember it real well almost like yesterday because we both got these new baby-doll pajamas which are real terrific and we get to giggling in front of the mirror and doing like these dance numbers from the old movies and talk about how much we look like twins which we're often mistaken for by lots of people even who know us real well when we dress alike. Well, later we make these real great sundaes with a whole quart of Sealtest French Vanilla and Smucker's Fudge Sauce and peanuts and stuff and we're sitting just sitting there in the kitchen and the newspaper is there on the table where my folks had left it when they went away in the morning and we're not really even looking at it but we sort of look at it I guess and here's this ad for go-go dancers. I don't think we thought we'd get the job and we sure didn't know anything about show business except from movies but we thought it might be kinda fun to go to an audition and so that night and the whole weekend in fact we practised dancing and Becky Gae and I we both really love to dance. Like we could both go home from work with feet that were ready to scream from standing up on them all day and still we could go out and dance half the night. Crazy, huh? But that's how much we both love to dance, so it wasn't work to us and besides we had danced together just for fun ever since we were real little and even when we'd double date we used to dance sometimes together because we can really dance together better than we can dance with most guys, you know? We never missed a dance in high school and we like never even left the floor even if we had to dance with each other. So I guess dancing's just in our blood or something but we never expected to make careers of it or anything. That was on a Saturday night that we saw this ad in the paper and we practised that night and again all day on Sunday and Sunday night and in fact we didn't even go to mass on Sunday which I practically never miss and Becky Gae too. So Sunday night I called the number in the paper and we were both giggling so

much because of the whole idea of being go-go dancers which
we still didn't take seriously that I thought I wouldn't even be
able to talk but this man with this really nice business-like voice
answers the phone and then I got more serious and we made an
appointment for an audition on Monday afternoon—just like
that! Which meant of course that we both had to phone work
and say we were sick and so our parents wouldn't know we had
to leave home early anyhow just like we were going to work
like any other day and spend the whole day downtown and it
was like playing hooky which was fun but about lunch time we
both got this kinda nervous feeling or something. I mean I could
just tell it about Becky Gae without her even *saying* anything
which happens a lot and is really spooky and all of a sudden we
both started thinking what it really was to be in show business
and all. I'll just never ever forget how I was eating this hamburger and coke and Becky Gae a hotdog and coke when we got
to talking really seriously about it and about how we ought to
be billed and all and what kind of show business names and all
we ought to have and we both thought our names were real
good together—Sandra Mae and Becky Gae—but how could
you be in show business with a name like Golakowski which
was too hard for some people to say besides not sounding real
American. And then we both thought of it at the same time like
this thing came down out of the sky and wham! that we ought
to call ourselves the Golly Sisters. Maybe Becky Gae had said
something like, 'Golly, isn't it exciting?' or that kind of thing, I
don't remember, but suddenly we both thought of it—zap!
And that's what we are—the Golly Sisters. Which we also aren't.
Sisters, I mean. We're just cousins, but our mothers got pregnant
at like almost the same split second and went to the hospital at
the very same time and both had us just a few minutes apart and
our fathers being brothers and all and our just popping out into
the world at almost the very same minute and all they decided
to give us names like twins and used to dress us alike and all and
it was really like having a sister only maybe better. But boy were
we really nervous when we went to that audition. First we forgot
and walked right smack by Woolworth's and if anyone had seen
Becky Gae we would really have been in big trouble I guess
having called in sick and all. But that's how nervous we were or

maybe it was what they call stage-fright. Anyhow then we really got the creeps when we had to walk through this neighborhood with all these bars and everything and these drunks just standing around outside and making really very indecent rude remarks to us. I just can't believe that grown men drink beer and whiskey and stuff and get drunk in the daytime like that probably without having anything to eat. When I see men like that it nearly makes me want to puke or something. So it's a wonder we didn't just flop that audition feeling like that and never having done anything like show business before only seen some movies about it. And I guess maybe we wouldn't ever have gotten a start at all but just have gotten up on Tuesday morning and been a nurse's aid emptying doo-doo and a parakeet-saleslady also emptying doo-doo if it hadn't been that Mr. Jones was such a gentleman and made us feel so right at home right away and thanked us for coming and going to all the trouble and everything. He took us to the dressing room where we could change which felt kind of funny putting on baby-doll pajamas in the middle of the day but not having real costumes we thought maybe they would be alright which they were I guess since we got the job just like that. Mr. Jones put money in the juke box and helped us up onto this bar and Becky Gae and I both thought wow what if we just fall off or something but we can dance just about anywhere and have danced in some real crazy places and I guess we both forgot about being scared or feeling silly or something and just danced. Well the next thing you know all six records had played and we were really just warming up being used to dancing for hours and hours it not being work at all when you love it like that. Mr. Jones gave us both cokes and we sat at the bar with him which was the very first time we'd ever been in a bar and he explained about working six nights a week and what would our parents think and we said we were both free white and twenty-one which was not true being both twenty but he knew what we meant and he said fifty a week each just to start which was already a little better than selling parakeets or emptying bedpans and less hours and besides dancing which we both just love you know and maybe a chance for a career. And that was two years ago. Naturally our parents especially the fathers hit the ceiling and how and you

would have thought they wanted to put us in a convent or
something what a mess and screaming and shouting but we
explained and explained that we didn't have to take our clothes
off and that it could be a big start in show business and offered
both of us to put fifteen a week into the family kitty which
would still leave us if we were careful lots for clothes and 45's
and stuff. Well my father didn't believe the whole thing was for
real and thought we were being trapped in some kind of house
of prostitution or something so went storming down to see Mr.
Jones who is always a gentleman and so soft-spoken and told
him what natural talent we had and good rhythm and how he
would be personally responsible and everything. So our parents
agreed on a trial basis and Mr. Jones had said that too—on trial
for a month—and our fathers actually drove us to work and
waited for us which we thought was a scream like being movie
stars and having chauffeurs but which was also treating us like
kids which was the part we naturally didn't like one little bit.
But they got used to it and they got used to the fifteen a week
too I guess and then it was alright and we passed our trial and
worked up some good new dances with Chip the piano player
and really got some classy stuff into the act which I remembered
from ballet classes. That was two years ago. We don't live at
home any more but in this real cute efficiency apartment real
modern which is just big enough for us with one double bed
that makes a couch for when we have company and this real
nice kitchen when you fold back the doors only we usually don't
do much cooking. We've had some offers to do TV work and
advertising and stuff from guys who discover us in the bar and
are surprised we are working with our talent in a place like that
but so far not exactly what we think is the right offer because
we'd rather take it slow and not make any mistakes that might
hurt our future careers like Marilyn Monroe who was so beautiful I can't stand it did when she posed for those calendar pictures
which she was blackmailed for later. I say we need an agent but
Becky Gae she says I've got a good head for business and she'd
rather trust me and Mr. Jones always gives us good advice being
always a gentleman and very smart besides and having made a
nice little bundle I guess with the Melody Bar. Some of the other
girls who work there aren't exactly ladies and in fact are very

foul-mouthed with cursing and no better maybe than common prostitutes if you know what I mean. But they mostly don't stay but a few weeks and we get along real well with the regulars —with Chip and of course with Mr. Jones and with Joe the bartender and everybody and some of the girls who come through here are real nice even the ones that get kind of dirty when they're performing but are real ladies when they're not on stage. Tessie's our favorite who says she feels like a stage mother with us and gives us nice presents whenever she's here. Naturally sometimes we have trouble with some of the customers who would like to get fresh and put their hands on you and stuff and just make us want to puke. But most of the guys who come in are real nice and like college types and some real sharp dressers they are too some of them. And they're always real complimentary about our costumes which or almost all of which Becky Gae makes herself on our portable Singer which we bought almost right away after our trial period was over. She was always very handy Becky Gae being just about the best student always in all her Home Ec classes and having gotten the Future Homemakers of American brass plaque at our graduation which made me almost as proud as if I'd gotten it myself. And when she walked across the stage I kept thinking oh please don't let her trip or something awful which she didn't. We will both of us maybe someday take acting lessons which we will probably need if we really get serious about our careers which for the moment we aren't but are just kind of testing it even though of course show business can be very exciting with new faces and things happening all the time. People say don't you get tired of dancing like that and what they don't know but would probably find real funny is that not only do we not get tired of dancing but our very favorite thing to do on our night off when we have a date is to go dancing. We're really crazy about it and don't give a darned about anything else if we can just have some good music and a chance to dance. Chance to dance. Like a poem, huh? Which is no doubt the reason Mr. Jones made us regulars, like he says that we just turn our motors on and go and everybody can tell it's fun for us more than work even for two whole years. The only bad thing about going on in show business and becoming stars and maybe doing television or movies is that we'd not only probably have to give up this darling apartment but would have to also say bye-bye to Mr. Jones who is really like a father to us as I often tell him. And some people would probably have trouble understanding that on account of the fact that to some people he probably seems kind of strange with that sick little arm of his but it's what's inside that counts. That's what I think when some of these really prostitute-like dancers come here and use foul language and all that Becky Gae and I aren't even touched at all by that because if your spirit is a pure and shining light it shines even in that foul darkness and so we should not despair. Also we now make seventy-five a week which is not chicken feed and also sometimes tips which it is not necessary to declare on your income tax being really like just getting little presents. Being still very religious of course we give seven-fifty per week to the church even if we don't always attend regularly because of being just too pooped after Saturday night which always seems very strenuous. Bye-bye, bedpans, that's what I say and Becky Gae says the same thing only about parakeets which are anyhow so darned messy throwing their food all over the place and making so much do-do that who would want one in his house anyhow is what I want to know.

13 Melody

The ticket was a rectangle of salmon pink pasteboard—the black-printed face glossy and smooth, the back dull and coarse. When he first tried to pluck it off the counter with his fingers it seemed to resist him, to cling to the polished marble as though it were glued down. He thought of the bright quarters of his boyhood—the ones glued to the hardware-store counter to trick the greedy. His fat, dull fingertips couldn't lift the card, so he slid it forward until it tipped over the edge of the counter, and then caught it up in his palm. It was the winning ticket at last, and the address where he could claim his prize was clearly printed—222 East 222nd Street. It was late. He would have to hurry. City blocks were longer than he remembered, and they seemed to lean even farther apart as he walked. He imagined the city's grid from above, swelling and stretching itself out like some gigantic growth that consumed the surrounding countryside, growing fatter, taller, distances bending away into space. And he had forgotten how strange the numbering was. He stood in the crowd that waited at East 110th Street, moved on past the jewelry salesmen with silver springs and coils spread on velvet rugs lining the sidewalks, past apple-sellers and vast bright cubes of department stores and came to 113th street, and then farther, past garden supply stores, tire stores, drug store windows fat with beach toys, to 111th Street. The pump of his heart stepped up its pace, and he felt its echo hammer in his chest, rise to his head and swell the arteries at his temples. As panic sifted over him it was trapped between layers of coal soot and grit, making it harder to move, making his heart pump even faster. The small rectangle of pasteboard softened and melted into eucharistic pulp in his hand. What if no one could read it? What if they didn't believe he had really won the prize this time? He couldn't bear to look at the card again. Sweat filmed his eyes and mingled with the tears that began to wash his cheeks. He stumbled, pushed past a pair of ancient ladies, bent and twisted as tenement plumbing, and hurried on, half running, to the next corner: East 199th Street. And the next: East 200th Street. And the next: East 210th Street. His body now seemed dead from the waist down, and he knew only by the blurs of shop windows that he was actually moving, hurling himself ahead to the next intersection, trembling on the edge of the curb as he waited for the blur of red light to shift to green, and then plunging on, the ticket so much paste against his palm, his head flowering with the surges of blood that flung themselves against the raw linings of his brain. And then he stopped in disbelief, slowly squinting his eyes to make out each number in its turn: two; two; two. Two . . . two . . . two. Twotwotwo. East 222nd Street. Each number was a wisp of vagrant fog against the dark night of the street sign. He squinted again: two . . . two . . . two. Quickly he turned to the right. There was no number on the apartment house. He ran into the vestibule and checked the mail boxes. Nothing. And then he saw a magazine—a dusty tongue thrust from a broken box, and he drew it out: Emma Goldstein, 210 East 222nd Street. So he was near. He hurried down the steps of the building, turned right, and moved past a vacant lot cluttered with the insect forms of rusting baby-carriages and abandoned cars, then an empty building with the front door nailed shut and a cotton banner merrily flapping the red message: CON-DEMNED. The house number must be hidden beneath the banner. He rushed on to find the numbers on the next building washed away by rain; another with neat little porcelain numerals that had been shattered and hung like icicles in unreadable fragments. Then, down a short flight of stairs, he saw a shop window. He turned quickly, ran ahead, and slipped on the top step, slid forward on some anonymous vegetable decay and caught himself so sharply with his right arm that he felt the weight of his stopped body tear at muscle tissues. The pink card dropped soundlessly in a lazy downward fluttering into the paper-cluttered space before the shop window. On his hands and knees he searched through the litter, finding a used rubber, a damp package of cigarette papers, the crossword puzzles of shredded letters, a photograph of a man and woman with their heads torn away. And finally his hand lighted on the card. He held it up to catch the single, weak ray of sunlight that timidly penetrated the twilight gloom; yes, he could still read the address, and though the letters had begun to bleed away, the GRAND PRIZE WINNER stamp was still visible. His body heaving now to scoop in the air, he stood for a moment with his head pressed against the cooling glass of the shop window, and as his vision cleared he saw row on row of prosthetic limbs—arms sheathed in plastic skins, a chrome leg sprouting a wilderness of tangled straps and buckles, a taut black leather hand with its palm cupped upward. He pushed himself away from the window as though these parts might conspire to become a single being that would hurtle through the glass to attack him, and as he staggered back he saw the number on the window: 198 East 222nd Street. He had taken the wrong turning. He had all along been searching in the wrong direction. He should have turned left at the corner instead of right. Time was running out, and he began to cry, astonished at the piercing, animal loudness of his own voice, as he rushed up the stairs and began to run along the street. If his heart burst with the running, it was alright. This time he would win. He felt the paunch of his stomach rise and fall as he ran, the card clutched tightly in his hand, as he dodged between cars that bleated and screeched to a halt when he bounded across the intersection. Then he had his first glimpse of the building where the street took a sudden bulging curve—its bright neon sign flashing the numbers: 222. This time he would make it, and maybe his stomach humping like that against the air really helped, helped clear the way for his body, tunneling through space toward the bright window where the boy stood blonde and fair and waiting for him to present his ticket and claim his prize. If he only hurried. If only there were time enough.

Like film snapping apart, stretched too tightly against the sprockets of a projector, the dream ended, but Melody scarcely registered the difference between sleeping and waking: both states were now like a distantly throbbing toothache, heavy with the threat of worse pain to come. The pills didn't help. Somehow he had gotten through the desert of Wednesday, staring down into the closed, locked bar while daylight hours dragged into night and confidence struggled with fear as he tried to believe that Dixon would find some way to come back, would at least telephone, that he would understand the plan and not leave him alone, perched here over the yawning emptiness of the darkened bar. And he made it through the first show on Thursday night; but by the beginning of the second show the effects of two sleepless nights bore down on him and his whole body felt clamped by panic. He sang badly—missing notes he had always reached for and plucked down effortlessly, and stumbling more than once over the microphone cord that seemed to snarl his legs. Afterwards he doubted that he could drag himself up the stairs, and when he did, and had half fallen into the damask chair, he felt he would never rise out of it again. He gazed through the green veil of the mirror as the last customers left, as Joe gave the Golly Sisters a farewell pat and locked up the bar, and continued to stare into its vacancy long after the lights were turned out, as though he hoped to surprise the phantom shapes and shadows should they stir with motion. When first light began to carve at the darkness, he started to drink—not desperately, but with slow determination, in the hope that sleep might finally come. When it didn't, he took two sleeping pills and eased back in the chair, his feet propped on a footstool. Each nerve in his body seemed to be awake, listening, waiting, even though he felt the cradle of his mind rock toward sleep, drifting over the edge of consciousness toward the dream in which he ran, breathless and panicked, the pink card clutched in his hand and fluttering in the air as he ran.

When he awoke he felt his sweat-soaked clothes binding his body, twisted under his arms, knotted against his back, and he began to tear them away. Standing, fighting to keep his balance, he dragged at his tie, tried to unfasten the buttons of his shirt and then ripped them away as he struggled to free himself so that he could breathe again. Naked except for his socks, he stumbled across the room and poured a drink, the amber column of liquor rising until it overflowed the cylinder of glass. With one more pill he might be able to sleep enough, just enough, to go on with the second show tonight—if not the first show, at least the second. He tipped a sapphire-bright capsule out of the bottle; then a second; and he washed them down with a quick, gagging swallow of Scotch. Then slowly, carefully, as though his body might shatter if he moved too quickly, he slid one foot before the other and moved back across the room to lower himself gently into the chair. Joe was opening the bar. So he had slept more than he thought. If Joe was opening up, then it was between 4:00 and 5:00, and he had only a few hours before the first show, but if he could sleep, really sleep, for just a while, if he could still for a few hours the pounding in his head, he would be alright. And Dixon would come back tonight. No, it was last night that he would come back. Tonight then. Dee had been back a whole day—no, two. Dixon would come back last night and understand everything but not tonight or last night and understand everything because tonight Dee would be there and tomorrow night too and Dixon would be closely wrapped in the cocoon of her perfumed hair and could not return to him but maybe he would.

It didn't matter, after all, because he had finally won, and the pink card was clutched in his hand and there was still time, and the shop window glittered before him and there was time this time and no problem this time about choosing, for the entire window stretching away for gleaming block after block was filled with rows of smiling Dixons all beckoning to him. He rushed ahead and stood before the door, his body trembling with exhaustion and longing. A doorman blocked his way. 'Lemme see your ticket,' he demanded. The doorman was tall, lanky, with stringy muscles and hair greased back into an elaborate pompadour. He wore dirty levis, motorcycle boots and a t-shirt that freed his arms to display the crude, purple arabesques of tatoos. Where had Melody seen him before? How often had he seen him before? 'Lemme see your ticket,' the doorman snarled again. 'Ticket? My ticket?' Yes, the ticket. He slowly, proudly extended his arm to show the winning ticket, curled his hand open and offered the moist pink ball that he had squeezed tight in his fist. 'That ain't no ticket!' As Melody watched the ball shook, trembled, unfolded itself and spread lightly feathered wings. With a quick leap it fluttered away from him. 'No ticket, no prize!' the doorman snarled as he rattled a steel-mesh grating down between them. But it wasn't too late and he had a ticket and this time he would win and if he had no ticket it no longer mattered. Dixon beckoned from the window, and beckoned again and again down endless rows of Dixons and he rushed forward to meet them, arms outstretched to embrace them, and flung himself forward, his heart a song of adoration, into the waiting arms that would comfort and heal him.

14 Sammy

Well, treasure, let me tell you that that's one hard act to follow. I mean it's like coming on at the Palace *after* Judy Garland trying to follow that little number. Melody finally got his big break I guess. Ha-ha. I mean she just came sailing through that big trick mirror—and I do mean *trick*—like Dumbo playing Peter Pan and splash all over the bar and it was just horrid-horrid*horrid* with all that gooey blood and those broken bottles and mirror and all that perfectly luscious Martell just floating away. There was an old wino at the end of the bar who comes in perfectly stinking almost every time I'm there and he just belched and finished his beer and left like it wasn't anything at all to have a ton of flesh come flying through the air and go *splat* right in front of you but just part of the floorshow. I wish I had had a camera with me it was all so gooey and horrible and so tacky, dear. Nothing on. Not one stitch but her socks and I always think it's so nasty to see someone with just their socks on. It's so Polish! Did you ever get in bed with a trick and sort of snuggle down and then all of a sudden your feet touch his feet and you discover he's got on SOCKS? That just turns me right off, honey. I mean, he can be *the* most gorgeous number in the *world* and have socks on and turn me right off. It just makes me go limp. You know where! But you would not absolutely would not believe how pukey that number was in the bar. He looked just like ground beef you know—good ground chuck maybe. The flying meatball. N.A.S.T.Y.—that's what it was. And now the big mystery honey is did he fall or was he pushed or did he jump. It's just like Perry Mason or something and they want *me* to testify—me, imagine that? Now can't you see it with me in some little black dress that I keep tugging down over my knees: Yes your honor. No your honor. I don't know your honor. Or do they have your honors at inquests? Well it just makes me sick and why should I give up a whole day just to talk about Miss Meatball? I mean how am *I* supposed to know if she jumped or was pushed or whatever except that I can tell them I know she used to have some pretty rough trade up there because I've *seen* some of the numbers he used to buy and there were some real roughies there. Oh, honey, it may turn you on but those guys can really do you some *damage*. I had this rough number once who fucked me with this big rod until I thought I'd just *split* and he just wouldn't stop and wouldn't turn loose and squeezed this lovely bod of mine so hard I had bruises on me for three whole *months* and couldn't even *appear* on the beach it looked so awful and soooo tacky. If it turns you on that's O.K. I guess, whatever gets you off, but honey I wouldn't want to risk some of those numbers Melody used to drag back with her. That kind is pure suicide. And of course that may be what it was, too, that he just jumped right through that glass glory hole of his. She was so lovesick, Melody, over this very ordinary and very stuck-up little prick tease that I saw through in about five seconds. Now what did he ever think some young boy like that would see in him anyhow—a father figure? Maybe a mother figure. I mean nobody in his right *mind* is gonna want to do it with a freak like that unless there's plenty—P.L.E.N.T.Y.—of M.O.N.E.Y. in it for him. So what I figure dear but this is of course *quite* off the record is that this little hotcha, this very stuck-up trick, figures he's got a good thing going and plays up to Melody while his wife's away and Melody thinks it's for real and then the kid puts the squeeze on him and Melody says no or just doesn't *have* that much money and there's a big fight and Melody who is anyhow a very depressive type or was goes and throws himself through the mirror. But how am I supposed to say all *that* at an inquest? I mean, then I've got to say I know *all* about her sordid sex life and *how* am I supposed to say *that*? I mean, I've got a reputation to think about in this town, don't I? Well, it's all just too sordid. S.O.R.D.I.D. Don't you think? I mean who would ever think that she could pull a number like that? I mean, treasure, we all *knew* she was a little kinky but that's really too much—even if you *are* a masochist. I just can't describe to you what it was like. First of all I shouldn't even have *been* there and *wouldn't* have been there except by just the most silly chance. I hadn't been there for *weeks* in fact because she was being sooo evil and snotty about this little pussy that she wouldn't even have *known*, my dear, if *I* hadn't brought it in one day practically like *room* service or something. This really conceited little prick-tease—sooo grand! And I wouldn't have gone in at all except that I went for a fitting for this dreamy new cream-colored flannel lounging suit which you're just going to *come* when you see and Mario was of course out and I thought just one little drinkee while I wait. So there we are—me and this scabby drunk and Joe playing Miss Housewife scrubbing the bar and all of a sudden it's BOMBS AWAY! and this horrible noise of glass breaking like *nothing* I've *ever* heard *before* and flying through the air he comes—our own Wonder Woman looking for a secret plane, and *splat* onto the bar and *bounce* onto all those rows and rows of bottles and then it's so quiet you can't be-*lieve* it and this great piece of raw meat bleeding from every ugly pore and with his socks on which was putrid. But she was bound to come to a bad end, that one. I mean, treasure, she had been absolutely *courting* disaster from the word GO. Those rough tricks she always rented, and truck drivers and sailors. She used to go down on anything. Why, I caught her myself in the Greyhound Bus Station blowing this big ugly nigger who would probably just as soon have *stabbed* her. She had absolutely no taste in anything, but then I guess you don't have much choice when you're deformed like that. Can you imagine waking up and finding that arm of his—that *thing*—lying in your face? Vomit. So he *had* to pay for it of course, but he didn't have to drag in all that rough trade. I think that was probably suicidal anyhow, and who would really want to *live* looking like that? All I have to do is get a bad *pimple* and I can hardly face the world, and when I look in the mirror I think OOOO, I just want to *die* before I have to go out looking like that. But imagine if you have this Frankenstein arm and all. Well, it took some nerve to get up on that stage and dance all around like the sugar-plum fairy with that ugly thing flopping around. It used to make me so sick I thought I couldn't even come *into* the place but you learn not to look at it and where else in this crummy town are you ever going to *meet* anybody? I think it's just disgusting the way this crooked police force and this crooked mayor who is anyhow just a big Polack with white socks can do anything they want to and suppress things that are really quite normal and healthy. Why, they act just like homosexuality was some kind of sickness and not something that's been done by some of the greatest men in the *world*—like Plato and Richard the Lion Hearted and maybe even *Jesus* who after all never married and lived with all those *men*. I mean, if they'd ever *read* something instead of just fucking every available pussy they can find they'd be a little more en-*light*-ened. That kind of prejudice is sooo stupid and it makes life very hard for people who just want to be themselves. That's the reason I don't even want to have anything to *do* with this inquest. City Hall sucks, honey, and I won't even drive my *car* past it. And who cares? Pushed? Shoved? She's just one big piece of hamburger now anyhow and who really *cares* how she got that way? I think the whole thing's just *stupid* and just because I happen to be unlucky enough to be *standing* there minding my own business when it happens is no reason I should have to give up a whole *day* and maybe even compromise my own reputation in this town. The town may suck but it's where I make my *living*, you know. But she certainly went out with a *bang* and maybe it's better than being knifed by some drunk nigger or strangled with your nylons. She could be *sooo* tacky. Her middle *name* was tacky. Anyone who would come out in that gold lamé outfit with that little arm flapping around must have *invented* the word tacky, and trying to do that Streisand number with that awful frog voice of hers. Super-tacky, that's what it was. Well you just *know* that somebody who would do things like that just couldn't have any *taste* and especially not with those mean tricks of hers. Frankly, I think she was probably just a size queen anyhow except that her little stuck-up boyfriend the prick-tease probably didn't have much in *that* department. All potatoes and no meat—that's my guess. Maybe that's what got through to Melody, finding out the kid had his thumb on the scale when he weighed in. Ha-ha. Now I think big ones can be V.E.R.Y. stimulating but I also know it's not the size of the *wand* that makes the magic of the magician, honey. It's a question of appreciating the *art* of the thing, right? Well, I can't imagine she had an ounce of art in her—just fat: F.A.T., fat all over and also in her *head*. Living the way she did she was just *asking* for trouble and especially since you could just *tell* from the way she cried during some of those numbers she sang that she was a really sloppy romantic. I mean you can't be a *size* queen and after rough trade all the time and so ugly you have to *pay* for it and also be a romantic. Now that is *really* suicide is what it is. You're talking to somebody who knows, sweetie, because I've been in love *dozens* of times but I'm not some side-show freak and I don't *pay* for it either. If some trick so much as *mentions* money to me, I send him to the nearest employment bureau. There's enough dick around without having to *buy* it. That really makes it degrading, you know? And I suppose you've got to feel sorry for somebody whose life is so degraded and everything and can't *help* being a freak like that, but then he ought to know better than to try to make it with a cute young number like that even if the cute young number *is* after all just a big prick-tease. She was way out of her class, honey—*miles* out of her class when she started fooling around with something like *that* and I guess she probably got *just* what she was asking for. Maybe some rough trade threw her through that mirror because she sure didn't *fall* through because when it happened she was like shot out of a *cannon*, my dear—real gang-busters. If I had a body that ugly—which I wouldn't but would diet like crazy *not* to—I wouldn't even want to be seen *dead* looking like that, and with socks on too it was just *too much*. But I am sooo tired of hearing about the whole thing and everybody and his sister calling up and asking the *silliest* questions and pretending that it really *mat*-ters to them and all which of course it doesn't one bit but they are simply so horny for some gossip in this town where nothing ever happens that they just can't stay away from the phone. Alfie who is so *ungenerous* that it is sickening even suggested that maybe we should make some kind of memorial. Me-*mor*-i-al? I said. Well maybe MacDonald's would like to buy the corpus delicti to put on top of one of those revolving signs as the biggest hamburger in the world. But the *worst* part is that everyone calls up and pretends to be interested in *you* even when you haven't heard from them in months and months and then they want to hear *all* the gory details and then suddenly they want to tell you all *their* troubles, and that's really *too much*. Trouble I can find and Ann Landers I am *not*. If you want sympathy, I always say, you can find it in the dictionary between 'shit' and 'syphilis'. Some people have a terrible nerve, imagining everybody is interested in their problems and has time to *listen* to them. No thanks honey, Sammy has her *own* fish to fry thank you and certainly doesn't need to give up a whole *day* to go sit on some fucking hard bench at City Hall and then have to tell about the great hamburger that came flying out of the sky like the bleeding saints in those awful paintings. Religious art always *did* seem to me so morbid with these half-naked men all chopped up and if I will absolutely nevernever-*never* go into a museum to see such morbid things, what have I done to deserve to have one come flying at me when I'm simply minding my own business and having a drink? It's an invasion of *privacy* is what it is! Let the saints bleed in someone else's fucking martini next time.